THE SHAKE UP

CAPRICORN COVE SERIES

EVIE MITCHELL

THUNDER THIGHS PUBLISHING

Editor: Nicole Wilson, Evermore Editing
http://www.evermoreediting.wixsite.com/info
Cover illustrations: Laras Putri

ALSO BY EVIE MITCHELL

Capricorn Cove Series

The Shake-Up

Double the D

Muffin Top

The Mrs. Clause

New Year Knew You

Double Breasted

As You Wish

You Sleigh Me

Resolution Revolution

Meat Load

Larsson Siblings Series

Thunder Thighs

Clean Sweep

The X-list

Reality Check

The Christmas Contract

Dogg Pack Books

Puppy Love

<u>Bad English</u>

<u>The Frock Up</u>

<u>Pier Pressure</u>

All Access Series

Knot My Type

Love Flushed

Nameless Souls MC Series

<u>Runner</u>

<u>Wrath</u>

<u>Ghost</u>

<u>Shield</u>

Elliot Security Series

<u>Rough Edge</u>

<u>Bleeding Edge</u>

ABOUT THE AUTHOR

Evie Mitchell is a thirty-something romance author (she/her/hers) living with disability. She believes in inclusion, accessibility, and fierce romance. Her loves include steamy romance novels, her husband, their THREE sausage dogs (heaven help her), and her ever-growing collection of book-related mugs.

As a woman with a diverse work history including in areas such as emergency response, event management, human rights, disability access, and security - her books are filled with true stories (bridezillas), worst-case scenarios (malfunctioning dresses), and her favorite tropes (one-bed).

Evie specialises in fiercely inclusive happily ever afters.

ACKNOWLEDGEMENT OF COUNTRY

I acknowledge the Traditional Custodians of the lands on which I write, the Ngunnawal people, and pay my respect to elders both past and present.

I acknowledge the continued and deep spiritual relationship of the Australian Aboriginal and Torres Strait Islander peoples' to this land, and their unique cultural and spiritual relationships to the land, waters and seas and their rich contribution to society.

Always was, always will be.

As always to my husband. For being my one true annoyance.

And to one year of author-bliss thanks to my beautiful greedy readers.

HOLY SHIT! HOW DID THAT HAPPEN???

THE SHAKE UP

Anika

My milkshakes may bring all the boys to my bar, but that doesn't mean they wanna hang around for dessert.

Despite being the perfect woman – attractive, confident and a world class chef – I'm not marriage material. I've resigned myself to that fact. But that doesn't mean I don't want a man in my bed.

And Mac? Or should I say, Mac-Daddy? Well, he's just the man I'm looking for.

Temporary.

Mac

Anika's convinced this is a short-term thing between us. But what she doesn't realize is she was mine from first glance.

If only I can convince her that we go together like salt and pepper, like meat and veg,
like... well, you get the idea.

Brace, Anika, I'm about to shake up your
world.

*Warning: This book is inspired by burgers,
eggplants and men who fight for what they want.
So, get thee a man, some whipped cream, and settle
in — this naughty little read will have you asking
for seconds.*

1

Anika

"Wait, we're doing what?" I placed my knife on the cutting board, leaning heavily against the countertop as I stared at my younger sister in shock. "Say that again?"

Farrah sighed heavily, pinching the bridge of her nose as she repeated the bad news. "Kapil's booked a cruise for Mom and Dad. He expects us to split the cost."

"He did this without asking us?"

"Ani, when has our brother ever asked for permission?"

I blew out a breath, shaking my head. "That's true." I mentally tried to recall my bank balance, wondering where I'd find the cash.

"Maybe we can talk him out of it," I said desperately. "If we catch him—"

"It's already done, Ani." Farrah dropped her hands, pressing her palms to the countertop. "Our brother is an idiotic, inconsiderate dickwad. And now we have to pay for it."

"Or, and go with me here, we could just not," I said, holding my hands up in an exaggerated shrug. "We could let him just own this shit and go with what we originally planned."

"So, we split a massage voucher between us while he gets them a goddamned cruise?"

I threw my hands up. "We're both poor, Farrah. He's a fucking stockbroker. His wife is head of her own law firm. They can afford to drop twenty thousand on a vacation."

"Technically, with the split between us, it would only be six-thousand, six hundred and sixty-six dollars."

"Oh yes, that devil's number makes me feel all the better." I picked up my knife, returning to viciously hack at the zucchini I'd been dicing for dinner. "And I'll note that it's not split between four but three. I mean, what the fuck, Farrah?"

She shrugged. "Well, technically, Chavvi is only the daughter-in-law, so—"

"Nope," I gave a vicious thump of my knife, taking an unhealthy pleasure in how the zucchini pieces flew across the bench. "Don't excuse them. If they're gonna make this decision for us, then they deserve to take equal responsibility for the consequences." I paused, shaking my head hard enough to send my straight black hair flying. "They know we're both on a tight budget. This is a selfish play."

Unlike Kapil, who'd bailed out of Capricorn Cove at the first opportunity, Farrah and I were lifers. I'd bought into the local bar with a friend, Ella Bronze—soon-to-be Ella Larsson—while Farrah ran the local wildlife preserve in addition to being the town's mayor.

Her job didn't pay much (translation next to nothing), and I'd used most of my savings on the bar. I was slowly building up a nest egg to buy a house, but that would take time and certainly didn't need the dent this cruise would make.

I didn't regret investing in the Bronze Horseman with Ella. The bar had started to turn a tidy profit for both of us. But that didn't mean I had cash to just throw at my parents for their anniversary.

"Call him," I told her, laying the knife down on the counter and scooping the remnants of the decimated zucchini into a bowl. "We need to tell him exactly where he can shove his pompous, presumptuous ass."

Farrah sighed, begrudgingly pulling her phone out as I began to aggressively grate a carrot.

Stupid brother.

"He's not gonna like us calling him during the day," Farrah said, nervously twisting on her bar stool as she fiddled with the phone in her hand.

"Tough titties," I barked, beyond incensed by this ridiculous scenario. "He got us into this mess, he's getting us out."

The phone rang four times before he finally picked up.

"What?" Kapil asked, his tone brisk. "I'm busy."

"Well, hello to you too, brother," I called saccharinely, my body tensing.

Calm, Anika. You know he won't respond well to aggression.

"Anika," he greeted flatly. "What do you want?"

"We're just calling about Mom and Dad's gift," Farrah started, her voice soft and halting.

"It's too much," I said, cutting to the chase. "We can't afford it. Farrah and I are on tight budgets, and you made this decision without asking. We're happy to pay a little toward it, but a three-way split isn't gonna happen."

"So, you think their fortieth anniversary isn't the time to splurge on them?" he scoffed.

"That's not at all what I said," I absently picked up my knife, twirling it in my hand. "We're happy to contribute to a joint gift. But neither of us can afford this cruise."

There was a pause. "Then get a loan."

Farrah's gaze locked on mine, her eyes wide and terrified.

"That's unacceptable."

I could feel his scorn dripping down the line. "If you'd both made something of yourself, this wouldn't be an issue."

And if you weren't such an ass, we wouldn't be in this predicament.

I made a mental note to look up voodoo dolls on Etsy.

"Kapil," Farrah started, her tone pleading. "What if we agreed to pay five thousand towards it between Anika and me? Yes, that means you and Chavvi need to take on the bulk of it, but you really should have asked us before committing us to such a large financial investment. You wouldn't do that to your clients, you shouldn't have done that to your sisters."

There was a pause as his pea-sized brain tried to process her gentle rebuke.

It was rare, but my meek sister sometimes dealt killing blows.

"Fine, we'll take on the bulk of it – but you need to tell Mom and Dad that."

In unison, Farrah and I rolled our eyes.

"Sure," I answered with a shrug. "When do you need the money by?"

"End of next month."

We both choked.

"N-n-next month?" Farrah repeated. "You need five grand by next month?"

My gaze flew to the calendar magnet stuck on my fridge, rapidly calculating the days. Fifty-four days to raise two-and-a-half thousand.

How?

"But—"

"Look, I don't have time for this. If you need anything, call my PA." He hung up, the call disconnecting.

Farrah slowly reached for her phone, switched it off and tucked it back into her pocket. Silence dominated the room as we tried to process what had just happened.

"I could... get another job."

I shook my head. "You're already working two jobs, babe. You shouldn't need to do more. Just ask the town to pay you a wage."

Our town's population had been minuscule for so long that there'd been no money to pay the mayor a wage. But as work from home grew more common and people decided they wanted to move to smaller, more affordable towns, Capricorn Cove had experienced a population explosion.

But some of the old ways stuck – including the one where the mayor did all the duties without seeing a dime.

Farrah bit her lip, shaking her head. "The re-election is coming up, and Dawson Hobbs is running. He wants to undo the protections for the wildlife preserve and bulldoze it to make room for condos and a resort." She blew out a long breath, the gust catching one of her curls and sending it flying. "The last thing I can do is ask for payment. He'll find a way to use it against me."

I wracked my brains for answers. "We might have some extra shifts at the bar I could get you. I'll have to ask Ella, but we could try."

She smiled, but it was thin and strained. "Thanks."

Farrah jumped off the stool, pressing her hands to her lower back and arching. "I need to get back. We're on hatchling watch tonight."

Hatchling watch involved spending most of the night walking up and down the coastline looking for baby turtles as they emerged from their buried clutch. When the little cuties appeared, Farrah would tag a few for scientific purposes before helping them and others crawl down the beach and into the waves. Her life re-volved around their protection and while I loved that she had found her passion, I just wished it paid more than the pittance she accepted.

"Wait," I turned, finding my purse to pull a voucher free. "At least use this since there's no point in giving it to the parentals now."

She took it, her lips curling into a wry smile. "You sure?"

"Positive," I pulled my younger sister close, wrapping her into a hug while silently cursing my brother for the additional pressure he'd placed on Farrah's shoulders. "We'll work it out."

"I know. We always do."

She left, and I returned to the kitchen, sud-denly not in the mood to make the zucchini slice I'd been planning for dinner.

You need a pick me up.

I glanced at the clock, noting the time. It was my rostered night off and normally I'd be crashed out on the sofa binging all the shows I'd missed while pulling the late shifts. It was exactly what I'd planned before Farrah had ar-rived with news delivered straight from the devil.

I tapped my nails on my granite countertop, considering my options.

Stay home and let Kapil ruin my viewing of

The Last of Us with his pigheadedness or go out and work off this angst with a Pedro Pascal stand in?

If I rushed then it was still early enough that I could head to the city before the pickings got slim I'd be left with the drunks and creeps.

A one-night stand with a willing man I'll never see again?

I grinned, reaching for my fridge door to store the zucchini.

Just what the chef ordered.

2

Mac

"Yeah, the tires on both sides blew so I'm holed up until I can get a replacement tomorrow," I told my best friend and boss as the cute waitress slid a tall glass of cider across the bar. She gave me a wink, then skipped off to serve the next customer.

"Do you want me to come pick you up? It's only an hour and a half drive," Gunnar asked. I heard movement in the background and the jingling of keys.

"Nah, I'm good. The tow guy said the mechanic has the tires in stock. I'll be back on the road tomorrow."

"You sure?"

I lifted the glass to my lips. "Positive. By the

time you get here, it wouldn't even be worth heading back, we'd just be sitting around waiting for the mechanic to open."

"Okay man, I'll see you tomorrow."

"Have a good night, and tell Ella hi for me."

"Will do."

We hung up, and I took my first long drink. The bar took up half the ground floor of the hotel. An older establishment, it wasn't exactly my usual scene. Fancy and expensive with a ridiculous number of businessmen in suits and ties and women wearing a mix of corporate and cocktail.

I looked down at my worn jeans and grinned.

It's a wonder they allowed me in with these dusty boots.

"Excuse me, is this seat taken?"

The low voice held a hint of a crisp British accent.

I glanced over my shoulder and immediately felt my body react.

Yes, please.

Slim with long dark hair that she'd brushed into generous waves, her lips were a full delicious red that reminded me of hot nights and sweet cherries. Her clothing was also siren red, a little crop top that tied just under her small breasts with a high-waisted long skirt that would have looked almost chaste if not for the thin band of skin at her waist and the split along one side that showed her leg right up to the top of her thigh.

Is she wearing panties?

"No," I finally choked out, shifting slightly to give her more space. "No one's using it."

She flashed a smile that reached her dark eyes, and my world tilted.

Well fuck a duck and feather me with tar.

She placed her small clutch on the bar and reached for the drinks menu, pursing her lips as she considered the options.

Say something!

"You come here often?"

I cringed, hearing the stereotypical pick-up line coming out of my mouth. In an effort to minimise damage, I gestured down at my clothes. "Obviously, I don't. Didn't realise I'd missed the dress code by a couple of levels."

She laughed, dropping the menu to swivel slightly toward me. "This is my first time. I'm only in town for the night."

"Work?" I asked, trying to flag the bartender down to get her a drink.

"Something like that." She nodded at my beer. "Is that the house cider?"

"Good eye. It's not bad."

She reached for my drink. "May I?"

I nodded, watching as she lifted it, turning the glass until her lips touched where mine had been moments earlier.

My cock went rigid in 2.5 seconds.

"Mm." She set the glass back on the wooden bar top, licking her lips. "You're right, it's quite good."

I had to look like a fucking idiot as I gawked at her, shifting on my seat to try and hide the fact a certain part of me enjoyed this way too fucking much.

Don't read into this. Don't be a fucking creep. Don't read into this.

"Have you ordered?" she asked, lifting the food menu and beginning to read.

"Nah, figured I'd have a drink then order some room service."

She lifted an eyebrow, giving me a teasing smile. "Is that an invitation?"

Fuuucccck.

I took a gamble. "You want it to be?"

Her gorgeous eyes drifted from my face and down my chest, her eyelashes fluttering for a moment as she caught sight of my erection.

"I think I do," she murmured, her body drifting toward mine.

The bartender arrived, looking a little frazzled. "Another?" she asked me with a harried smile.

"Yeah, and we'll get..." I looked at the woman, raising an eyebrow, inviting her to order.

"A margarita."

The waitress nodded and bustled away while I considered the stunning woman beside me.

"I'm Mac, by the way." I held out a hand, using it as an excuse to touch her.

She slid her palm against mine. "I'm Ani."

"Annie," I repeated, liking how her name tasted on my tongue.

"Here you go." The bartender slid our drinks across the wood. "Add it to your room tab?" she asked me.

"Please."

She hurried away, rushing to serve the next customer. The bar had gotten louder and more crowded as the Friday night business rush converged with those looking to hit the town.

I lifted my glass, tilting it Annie's way. "To new friends."

Her lips quirked up into an attractive smile. "I'll toast to that."

We clinked our glasses together, both of us taking a long drink. She pulled the glass away from her mouth, leaving a gap in the salt and an imprint of her lipstick.

I wanted to see that cherry red shade decorate my cock.

"So," Annie said, her tongue darting out to catch the salt crystals sticking to her glorious lips. "You mentioned room service?"

The desire that has been crackling through my veins ignited, burning through me, and chasing away any thoughts of reason.

"I'm in room 908." My voice was unrecognizable, rough with need and growly with want.

Annie slid from the barstool, her skirt catching on the seat, sliding higher to reveal her tawny thigh.

All that glorious skin, perfectly bared for me.

Room. Now.

She tipped her drink back, downing it quickly before turning away. With a flick of her hair, she shot me a saucy grin over her shoulder. "Shall I lead the way... Mac?"

I liked the way my name sounded coming from between those lips.

I followed her from the bar and across the lobby to the elevator. Our bodies brushed as we stole glances while waiting for the cart to arrive.

"Phew! Busy night in there, isn't it?" A man appeared beside Annie, shaking his head.

We both nodded, making affirmative sounds. The tension between us was thick and built as we waited. I embraced it, aware of the way my body had begun to tune into hers.

Our breathing matched. Our hands drifting close to each other but not touching. Our gazes caught, held, then drifted away only to catch once more.

"You two here on business or pleasure?" The man asked as the elevator reached the lobby, a group of chattering couples spilling out.

"Pleasure." I barked, capturing Annie's hand to pull her in. "Appreciate if you'd catch the next one. I need to kiss my girl."

The guy froze mid-step, then stumbled backward, stuttering, "O-o-of course. Have fun!"

The doors slid shut as I crowded Annie into the back corner of the cart. Her big beautiful eyes widened, desire written across the lines of her face.

"Gonna kiss you here," I told her, my hands grazing the soft skin of her neck. "Then here." My hands drifted over her body and down until I cupped her pussy. She whimpered in response.

"When I get you in the room. Gonna take my time, gonna taste your cream on my tongue. Gonna make you come until you're soaked and begging for my cock. You good with that darlin'?"

She swallowed, her lips parting on a slight pant as she nodded.

Fucking brilliant.

I kissed her softly. Just a brush, a teasing taste to whet our appetites. Grains of salt still clung to her lips, the salt drawing me in. I liked her lips, murmuring my enjoyment.

With a wordless mutter, Annie exploded under my hands, her body sinking into mine, her arms wrapping around me, her fingers delving into my hair to pull me closer.

I let her, taking control of our kiss, the heat, the wet, the passion. She tasted of salt, tequila, and a note that I'd associate as being purely hers. Her taste intoxicated me, stoking my desire, and fueling this chemistry between us.

Never had I tasted something as deliciously decadent as this woman.

The bell chimed, and the doors slid open behind us. For a moment, I considered ignoring them. All I wanted was for this kiss to go on forever.

But Annie moaned, the sound so needy, so fucking innocently sexy that I lost all thoughts of kissing and instead determined that I needed to draw it from her once again—immediately.

I captured her hand and tugged her along with me down the carpeted hallway. Slid my card in door, I shoved it open, Annie following me like a lamb to the slaughter.

Good girl.

Kicking the door shut, I backed her up, crowding her against the door, my lips finding hers once more.

I couldn't silence my groan as her tongue tangled with mine. Her taste was just as salty-sweet and ten times more addictive now we were alone.

She is bliss.

3

Anika

Oh my God, this man can kiss!

Mac kissed like a man born to do nothing but make a woman's insides melt. He teased and stroked, devoured, and savoured.

I wanted his mouth on my pussy. *Now.*

My fingers tangled in the soft strands of his hair as I gently applied pressure, pushing him down. He drew back, resisting my attempt, and I noted with satisfaction his swollen lips and the red of my lipstick on his skin.

"You okay?" he asked, wild-eyed and rough-voiced.

"Oh yes," I grinned, satisfaction fuelling the

raging inferno of need inside me. "But I'm pretty sure you promised me something."

The grin on his face was ridiculously attractive. Mac wasn't good-looking in the traditional sense. He was far too rugged tp be considered handsome. He put me in mind of a Scottish laird, rough and ready for battle among the moors. Or perhaps a conquering barbarian, untamed and unashamedly masculine.

"I did," Mac agreed, pressing a kiss to my neck. "Let's move this to the bed."

I kicked off my heels and then lay down on the king mattress, watching as Mac considered me from the end of the bed.

"Like what you see?" I asked, raising an eyebrow.

He grinned. "Just working out where to start."

I pointed at my crotch. "Here is good." I drifted my fingers up my body, cupping my small but gorgeous breasts. "Or here."

His breath hitched, and I couldn't help but grin as he dropped to his knees. His hands reached up, clutching my ass and pulling me down the bed until my legs were able to be draped over his shoulders and my pussy was at the perfect level for his tongue.

"Brace," Mac ordered as he slowly glided my

skirt up my legs, over my thighs, to bunch at my waist.

He sucked in a breath, a growl escaping.

"Oops," I pushed up, biting my lip and giving him an exaggerated guilty look. "Did I forget to wear panties?"

Mac's answer was a feral curse as his head lowered until his mouth touched me. I flopped back on the bed, my eyes closing, my hands reaching out in desperation for a pillow to smother my cries.

All those visions of lairds and barbarians proved true – Mac didn't hold back. He sought to conquer me. His mouth was poetry, his tongue a symphony of movement as he plundered.

Dear God. Is this love?

Mac teased and taunted, playing my body beautifully.

"Fuck," I groaned into the pillow. "I'm gonna come."

He tugged the pillow from my grasp, staring up at me hungrily. "Let me watch."

He dipped his head once more, his talented mouth finding my clit.

"God-Jesus-Mary-Joseph-and-all-the-blessed-saints!" I cried, arching off the bed as my body fractured.

As my climax subsided, I was left with one thought – *now*.

I wanted Mac's cock in me. Now. I needed this goddamned ache to subside, this feeling of emptiness.

"Mac..." I begged, his name a plea on my lips.

In a fumble of fingers and limbs, we stripped his jeans, shoving them just far enough down that he could free himself. He roughly shoved up my top, taking my bra with it.

"Fucking beautiful," he growled, his big, calloused hands cupping my breasts. "You're fucking perfect, Annie."

I reached between us, feeling his rigidity. "You gotta condom, big guy?"

He shifted, reaching into his jeans to pull his wallet free. He tugged out a condom packet tossing his wallet away. Tearing the packet with his teeth, Mac arched his body, shifting to roll it on.

Holy fuck, that's hot.

He shifted back up, fisting his cock. "Ready?"

I nodded, tilting my hips to give him better access.

Mac guided his cock to my entrance, and I had to bite my lip as he began working himself inside me.

The man is thick.

"Fuck, Babe," he groaned, dropping to press a hot kiss to my mouth. "You're tight as fuck."

I whimpered as he worked his way into me. He was average length but thicker, so damned thick.

Perfect.

As he rooted himself in me, Mac paused for a moment, letting me adjust.

"You're... God, it feels so good," I whispered, feeling myself stretching to accommodate his girth.

"Ditto."

We both huffed out a laugh.

"Gonna move," he told me. I nodded, bracing, then melted as his movement set every nerve ending on fire.

"Holy Jesus, Mary and Joseph," I cried, my body arching up to meet his.

Mac picked up his pace, his big body dwarfing mine as we both descended into madness. Need rode us hard, the sexual chemistry between us burning hotter than a wildfire. As my orgasm burned through me, every part of me flushed, clenched, and exploded until there was nothing left but a husk of me and a man gasping for breath on top of me.

"Sorry," Mac said, rolling us both over to tuck me into his side instead of crushing me.

We lay like that for a moment, our skin and blood cooling.

After a long few minutes, I raised up, giving him a grin. "Look, you can kick me out if you want – I won't mind because, damn."

He grinned, the hand that had gently been stroking my back now pressed into me, keeping me against him.

"But I need to eat. And then, if you're interested, I'd be down for round two."

Mac executed what I can only describe as a half crunch, resulting in me on my back and him looming over me once more.

Impressive.

He brushed a stray hair from my cheek, his eyes dark and needy.

"Dinner first. Then," he reached down, cupping my still-wet pussy. "Dessert."

Oh yeah.

4

Mac

A week later

"Jesus!" I spun on my heel, turning my back on the scene in the kitchen.

"Mac!"

"Shit!"

"Oh my God!"

I heard a mad scramble as my best friend and his fiancé fumbled for their clothing. I wanted to say this was an unexpected incident, but I'd only been in Capricorn Cove for a week now, and this was the third time I'd walked in on them getting it on.

They were insatiable.

Lucky fucking bastard.

At least some of my annoyance could be attributed to the fact Annie had ghosted me while I'd been in the shower. She'd said she'd call for room service. By the time I'd realised she wasn't joining me, it'd been too late. She'd vanished.

The woman had rocked my world, fucked my brains out, ordered me breakfast, and then disappeared.

You should have asked for her number.

"It's safe," Gunnar called, amused.

"Or I can claw my eyes out, and we need never go through this situation again."

"Dude, get in here. I got a solution to that."

I lifted a hand to my face, spinning and peering through spread fingers.

Ella stood by the kitchen counter, pouring cereal into a bowl, her face bright red. Gunnar crowded her, and while dishevelled, they were both, thankfully, clothed.

I dropped my hand. "Guys, we really need to set some clothing boundaries if I'm gonna stay with you."

"About that..." Gunnar held up a mug in question. I nodded, and he moved, kissing Ella's shoulder before heading for the coffee pot. "I had an idea."

I slid onto the bar seat at the counter; Ella perched next to me but not yet meeting my gaze. Couldn't say I blamed her.

"An idea?" I asked, accepting his coffee offering.

"Mm, Ella?"

She cleared her throat, pulling at the neck of her robe. "It's not that we don't want you here, Mac. It's just..."

"You guys are in the honeymoon phase and want to fuck like rabbits without interruption?"

She flushed, but there was a small smile on her face as Gunnar laughed. "Something like that."

I nodded. "Continue."

She cleared her throat, absently stirring her spoon around her bowl. "My friend, Anika, has a spare room at her place. She's looking to rent it out. We thought, if you wanted to, no pressure or anything, but maybe you could take a look."

Anything was better than stumbling across my best friend boning his fiancé. There were some things a man did not need to see. His best friend's erection being the top of that list.

"An-nie-ka you say?"

"Ah-ni-kah," Ella corrected. "She's also my head chef. I thought you could swing by for lunch and meet her." The blush had faded, and she was back to her confident and cheerful self. "It'll be on me, as an apology for the rude awakening."

I laughed, nodding at Gunnar. "Feel like he

should be the one paying. He's the one letting it all hang out."

"Hey!" Gunnar turned, slapping his butt. "This is prime, grade-A meat, my friend. All the ladies want a bite."

"What ladies?" Ella asked, narrowing her eyes at him.

"None that matter," Gunnar answered, leaning across the countertop to place a kiss on her lips.

"Correct answer."

I couldn't feel anything but glad for my buddy. He deserved a woman who loved him as Ella did. I'd only met her once before agreeing to come down and stay for twelve months to help Gunnar get this workshop up and running.

I'd lived in Cape Hardgrave most of my life, having moved there when I was three. My earliest memory was of Gunnar and I chasing each other around a table leg. We'd been inseparable for much of our lives. When he'd announced he was moving to the Cove, I'd been pretty fucking shocked. For one thing, Gunnar was as solid as they came. The joke had been it would take an earthquake to shake him from his comfortable routine.

Instead, it had been a dodgy boat engine and a thunderstorm. One night in the Cove and he'd fallen for Ella. The bastard had found a house, bought the marina, and gotten engaged all within the last three months. They were waiting until the end of summer to hold their wedding – just under a year. For a man who moved slower than molasses, he'd sure turned out to be capable of moving lightning fast when it suited him.

Watching them together, how easy their love was, how they acted and interacted, I could see why Gunnar was so gung-ho about making this work. The fool loved her to distraction. And, thankfully, it was mutual.

"Where's she live?" I asked, cupping my mug.

"Just down from the marina. It's a small condo with two bedrooms and a study kind of area. It's not big, but it'll fit two people nicely."

"How much?"

Ella named a price, and I whistled.

"Phew, that's low. That price wouldn't even get you a corner of a dog house back home."

Gunnar chuckled. "This town's still an uncut gem. We get the marina up and running, set up the workshop, get the boat rentals, and start attracting some developers to redo that old resort, you watch. This place will be a gold mine."

That was the thing about the Larssons, they knew where to invest. It was like a sixth sense for them. And they invested not only in property or businesses but in people. People like me.

"Well, for that price, I'll take it," I told Ella. "Does she need background checks or anything?"

Ella waved a hand in my direction. "Nah, just come at lunch, meet her, and we'll go from there." She hesitated. "I gotta warn you, Anika can be a little... scary."

Gunnar coughed into his fist. "Understatement of the year."

"What? She a murderer or something?"

Ella shook her head, her mass of dark hair falling off her shoulders. "No, but she knows five hundred ways to kill you and then serve you up with a side of chowder."

"Excuse me?"

"She's a chef. Real handy with her knives," Gunnar answered, stealing a strawberry from Ella's breakfast bowl. She swatted his hand, poking her tongue out at him.

"Should I be scared?"

Ella considered me, tilting her head slightly to the side. "Not today."

Gunnar clapped a hand on my shoulder. "Don't worry about it. Tell her the food is great, and she'll let you live."

Well, that's reassuring.

5

Mac

I walked into the Bronze Horseman and immediately found myself reassessing my opinion of the Cove.

The Bronze Horseman looked like something out of a movie. There were booths, intimate tables and classy stools lining the bar. The clientele was a mix of locals on lunch and tourists. Beautiful woods and soft leathers were offset by bronze fixtures and navy and forest green highlights.

You could lift this place up and plonk it in any major city in the world, and it wouldn't be out of place.

This luxury contrasted sharply with the marina. To say the place was shit was an understatement. Neglected, run-down, and practically derelict in some areas left a lot to be desired.

The old fish market warehouse that Gunnar was planning to turn into the second store of his family's shipbuilding business wasn't much better. The shipyard back at Thor's Shipbuilding in the Cape was a pristine, tightly run machine. Every building, every tool, every inch was perfect.

Based on what I'd seen this morning, we were lucky the goddamned warehouse was still standing.

"It's not that bad," Gunnar said again, sliding onto the barstool.

"Gunnar." I ran a hand through my filthy hair. "There's water ingress, mould, rot, whatever steel is rusted to goddamned shit, not to mention the smell." I shook my head. "You'd be better ripping the whole thing down and starting again."

"You're just afraid of hard work."

"More like a staph infection," I muttered, picking up the menu. "What's good?"

"Everything," Ella answered, walking out of the kitchen doors and moving to lean across the bar to kiss Gunnar.

"Thought you and Ma were doing wedding

shit?" Gunnar asked her, leaning across the bar to kiss her.

Gunnar's parents were in town to help Ella with the wedding planning. And to check out the family's newest investment.

She accepted his kiss with a ready smile and then shook her head. "Alas, no. That new waitress didn't work out, so I need to pull the lunch shift."

"The one you had a gut feeling about?"

Ella nodded, rolling her eyes. "That's the last time I don't trust my gut when it sends up red flags." She sighed. "Anyways, we're gonna check out that photographer this afternoon."

She sent a grin my way. "Now, what can I get you?"

"Surprise us," Gunnar replied before cupping the back of her head and pressing another kiss to her lips, holding her for just a moment longer than was decent.

Ella stepped back, laughing and swatting at his hands.

"Mac, Anika's out back. The lunch rush is on, but she'll be free after if you wanna chat." She turned, pulling a tablet from the back countertop of the bar and handing it over. "These are pictures of the room and house. Feel free to browse."

I took the offered tablet and began to flick through as Ella bustled about, working the bar and the restaurant around us.

"It's busy," I commented to Gunnar, swiping through the photos.

"Yeah, Ella and Anika have worked hard to get this place off the ground. If I hadn't seen the potential here first, I would have probably tried to talk Ella into moving to the Cape with me."

I paused on the picture of the kitchen, laughing as I zoomed in. "Did you see this?"

I tilted the tablet Gunnar's way, laughing as he squinted at the screen.

"Is that...?" He burst out laughing.

"Yep, a vegetable dick."

On the counter was a distinctly shaped cucumber with two tomatoes strategically positioned at one end.

"Gods, we're so going to hell."

I said that, but the more I looked through the pictures, the more I found various dicks in each of the images. In the bathroom, the fogged shower had a subtle dick drawn into the condensation. In the bedroom, throw pillows were artfully arranged into a classical phallic position. I found myself laughing and scanning each image closely, trying to find the subtle cocks amongst the decor.

"Here you go." Ella slid two plates before us.

Stacked hamburgers with sting fries and a generous side of sauce. The smell alone had my mouth watering.

"Thanks, Valkyrie," Gunnar said, reaching for his glass of soda. "So, what'd you think about the room?"

"I'll take it." I placed the tablet on the bar, reaching for a chip. "Subject to Anika's thoughts, of course."

We ate, discussing Gunnar's plans for the warehouse and marina. He pulled up a map of the marina on the tablet.

"The docks are in good shape, probably because that is the only part that's profitable at the moment."

"The ramps need work. And we'll need to staff the office. When's the inspector coming to check the fuel wharf?" I asked, referring to the floating station where boat owners were able to refuel.

"Tomorrow. If it's in good shape – and I suspect it is based on the original assessment included in the sale inspection, then we could look at installing one of those twenty-four-hour machines. With the number of boats in the area that use it, it'd be worth the investment."

I stuffed the last bite of the burger in my mouth, fighting the urge to order a second. Not because I was still hungry, the portion sizes were more than generous, nope, it just tasted that goddamned good.

"The ramps, berths, and office are our immediate priorities. We need cash flow as we rebuild the warehouse. I've got a lead on a temporary building for us to use while the warehouse gets kitted out," Gunnar said, placing the tablet on the bar.

"What's the plan for the warehouse? How long are we thinking?"

Gunnar ran a hand over his mouth, shrugging. "Until I get the contractor quotes, I won't know for sure. But I expect six months."

I nodded, looking back down at the map. "It's gonna be a multi-year project."

"Yep." He clapped me on the shoulder. "You wanna hang around to see this through?"

"Not a chance."

He laughed, but I already felt on edge. I needed sawdust on my skin, metal shavings in my hair and the taste of salt on my lips. I hadn't trained to be a shipwright to sit around waiting for a warehouse to be ready.

I'd known what I was getting into when I'd agreed to move here. I just hadn't realised it would be this big of a job.

"It's already spring." I looked down into the remains of my soda, mentally sketching a project timeline. "Six months brings us to autumn. That's assuming all goes well. It's likely to be mid-late winter by the time the warehouse is up and running." I shook my head. "The apprentice might be trained, but are we gonna have enough to keep us occupied while the contractors pull this together?"

Gunnar nodded. "The warehouse is about fifteen minutes up the coast. It's near the ocean but not on it. Erik and I discussed it. Once you and I work up a plan for the marina and secure the contractors, we'll take on the smaller projects from the home base. That'll free the Cape team to work on our normal fishing vessel and luxury orders."

I tossed that over. "You sure your brother is okay with this?"

Gunnar chuckled. "Erik has enough on his plate."

I couldn't argue with that. Gunnar had four siblings – Erik, Liv, Astrid, and Rune. The family was big, loud, and loyal as fuck. They loved loud, and I admired them for that. Over Christmas, Erik had somehow become guardian to twin boys.

"And the apprentice?"

Gunnar had already started hiring locals he'd be able to train for launch.

"Gabby's fucking talented. She's accepted the offer to head to the Cape over the summer.

Once Erik says she's good to go, we'll bring her back down and put her to work."

I nodded as Gunnar's phone let out a cheery beep.

"Hold on a second." He pulled his phone from his back pocket, swiping at the screen. "That's family chat." He scrolled, then swore.

"What's wrong?"

He held up the screen showing a photo of a dead rat next to a stuffed toy.

"Jesus, please tell me that isn't the twins' room."

"Oh, it is." Gunnar hunched over the phone, his fingers flying as he shot off a message.

"Your Ma's gonna freak," I said, glancing around.

"Liv said she's on it, but...." Gunnar shook his head. "I knew he was struggling, but you know Erik, he's not one to bother others."

"Kind of like you, yeah?" I bumped him. "Tell him you and Ella will deal with your parents. It's the least you can do to help the guy."

He rubbed a hand over his face. "Shit, Mac. Have we made the right decision to stay here?"

I waved a hand around the restaurant. "You tell me. Your girl is happy, your family is supportive of this investment." I gestured at his phone. "Don't let one rat derail your life."

He nodded, exhaling, his gaze finding Ella.

As if sensing him, she glanced our way, smiling and blowing him a kiss when she saw him looking.

"I'd give that woman the world."

"I know." I rolled my eyes. "Now, pull yourself together and tell your brother you'll deal with the parents."

The lunch rush quietened while Gunnar played peacemaker with the family. Liv had already enacted a cleaning intervention in the form of a reality TV show – which apparently was a thing you did when you were a hotshot producer.

Go figure.

I didn't hear all the details, but it sounded like the Larssons had it sorted. If only someone had explained that to Jemma and Sune. Ma and Pa Larsson had arrived at the bar and were freaking the fuck out.

"Mac, go on through. Anika will be cleaning up, and you really don't need to be here for this." Ella told me, looking a little frazzled as Jemma began to sob into Sune's chest, distraught at the idea of her grandbabies living in 'squalor'. I'd seen Erik's house, the place may be a bit messy thanks to the twins, but the guy lived in a beach house that looked like it could appear in one of those fancy architectural magazines.

I took the escape, ignoring the glare Gunnar shot at me over his dad's shoulder.

"Good luck," I mouthed, not the least bit repentant.

I pushed through the thick doors that separated the kitchen from the restaurant and entered a different world. Gone were the muted lights and soft tones. White subway tiles, black flooring, and stainless steel dominated the space.

"Jack, can you add aubergines to tomorrow's order?" A woman called from the open door of a large cool room. "I wanna do roasted garlic carrot and aubergine with panko crumb as a side dish tomorrow night."

"You mean eggplant?"

"Yes, smartass!"

The kid grinned. "Yes, Chef." He turned, catching sight of me in the door.

"Sorry dude, staff only."

"Ella sent me in. I'm looking for Anika?"

"Just a second," came the voice from the cool room.

"Behind!" yelled a waitress, brushing passed me, empty plates stacked in her arms.

"Chef, table three send their compliments. And a tip." The waitress handed the plates off to an older woman who immediately set to stacking them in a crate, using a hand tap to rinse them off.

"Pop it in the—" the woman emerged from the cool room, our gazes meeting.

We both froze, bodies snapping to attention.

"It's you!"

6

Anika

Holy shit, I have a stalker.

I moved without thinking, snatching a knife from the nearby counter and brandishing it his way.

"Stand back!" I yelled, making a stabbing motion. "I'm not afraid to use this."

"Jesus fucking Christ!" Mac bellowed, stepping back, his hands coming up to show me empty palms. "I'm unarmed!"

There was a crash from behind me, likely Jack dropping plates in his effort to protect me.

I spared him a glance only to find him cowering behind Beryl, my dishy.

Some apprentice you are.

The doors behind Mac swung open, Gunnar, Ella and Gunnar's parents racing in.

"Anika, no!" Ella threw herself in front of Mac. "What are you doing?"

"Dealing with a crazy stalker," I retorted, waving my knife again. "Get away from him."

"What do you mean stalker? This is Mac. You know, Leslie Mackenzie? This is the guy that I was telling you about, the one who's interested in renting your room."

I faltered, glancing from Mac to Ella to Gunnar and then back to Mac.

"You're telling me this is just a nice little coincidence?" I asked Mac, keeping my knife steady.

Mack shrugged, lowering his hands, an attractive grin tugging at his lips. "Seems like it."

I glanced at the Larssons. "You said you know this guy?"

"Been my best bud since I was in diapers," Gunnar confirmed.

I narrowed my eyes. "He a stalker type?"

Gunnar and his family laughed.

"Not even close," Sune told me, still chuckling. "This guy runs like the wind at the first sign of commitment."

I hesitated for another moment, then lowered the knife. "Well, shit."

Ella twisted, glancing over her shoulder at

Mac before her head twisted, her hands coming to rest on her hips.

Uh-oh... I know what this means.

"I think you have something to explain, Ms. Sharif."

I shrugged. "There's nothing to tell."

Ella's face flushed her head practically exploding. "Anika!"

"It was a misunderstanding." I looked to Mac, begging him with my eyes to back me up. "Right?"

He shrugged. "Sure."

My best friend in the entire world looked fit to kill. "I'm invoking rule four."

I sucked in a breath. "Really? You really wanna do this?" I pointed at Mac. "Over *him*?"

Rule four was sacrosanct in our relationship.

My mother was a marine biologist, and my father was a doctor. My parents had moved our family to the Cove when I was ten, so Mum could undertake a five-year study on a type of endangered sea turtle that only lived in this area.

Being biracial could be particularly hard when you moved into small towns where you were one of only a handful of people in town—most of whom you were related to—who looked different.

Then I'd met Ella. We'd been the odd kids at school. Ella, because she was confident, outspoken, hilarious, and chubby; me, because I had an accent and looked different from the other kids.

During one sleepover when we'd been about twelve or thirteen, we'd set up our ten rules for a healthy friendship. Rule four required us to either disclose our secret or repay the other person with a service they needed in penance for refusing to share.

I tended to be a holdout. Ella always gave in. If we ever broke the terms, then the rule was our friendship had to end—immediately.

And neither of us had ever contemplated seeing if the other would let that happen.

"Absolutely." She crossed her arms, glowering at me as I awaited her terms. "Tell me, or you're making my wedding cake."

I tried to hide a smile. I'd already planned on baking her cake. I mean, my gods. It was my best friend's wedding day, no one else would make her cake with as much love as I would.

"And," she continued. "I want five tiers."

I winced, my resolve chipping just a little. "Whatever you want."

"And each layer will be a different flavour."

"Hey!" I protested, my back aching just

thinking about the amount of work that would entail. "That's gonna take me days to –"

"With a white chocolate lace decoration on one side and dark chocolate on the other. And I want two Viking figurines on top in a longboat."

"Ella, come on, be reasonable."

She huffed. "You gonna tell me what—" she flicked a hand between Mac and me, "—this is about or are you gonna make my cake?"

I swallowed, determined to win this round. "What flavours do you want?"

And then Mac interrupted our negotiation to throw kerosene on the fire.

"We met when I got stranded in the city. Had a drink. I asked her out, and Anika turned me down." Mac shrugged. "It's not a big deal."

I shot him a death glare that promised the kind of retribution that would end with him burning in hell.

"The city? When? How? Anika never goes to the city." Ella looked back at me. "Anika?"

I swallowed, "I had an appointment." The lie tasted horrible on my tongue, but it was easier than admitting I wanted a little nookie for my cookie.

And boy, did I get it.

"What appointment?"

"A... a boob-related appointment," I said, digging a deeper hole. A memory of Mac's mouth on my nipple while his thumb brushed the underside of my breast sent a pleasant thrill down my spine.

Technically you're not lying.

"Boob? What's wrong with your boobs?" Ella asked, beginning to work herself into a panic.

"Nothing," I said, trying to calm the situation. "Promise."

Her lips pressed into a thin line. "Fine. But you're still making my cake."

I grinned. "We both know one does *not* break rule four."

"Alright." Gunnar waded in, wrapping an arm around Ella and directing her back toward the doors. "Let's all go have a chat at the bar about Erik and this rat situation, and leave these two to discuss their living arrangements." He sent me a meaningful look over his shoulder. "Don't hurt him too badly, Ani. I need him."

I performed a little salute. "No promises, Viking."

He rolled his eyes but escorted Ella and his parents from the kitchen, leaving Mac with me and my crew.

I leaned a hip against the counter closest to me, crossing my arms and giving him a long, leisurely once over.

Dressed once again in faded jeans, this pair were dirty, like he'd been working and had just stopped for lunch. His shirt was black, and the Thor's Shipbuilding insignia over his left pec had long ago faded. He wore tan lace-up work boots, and for some reason, the sight of them ignited my body.

"When Ella mentioned she knew a Leslie who was looking to rent a room, I assumed you were a woman."

Mac grinned. "How very stereotypical of you, Anika. I'm shocked."

I felt my lips twitch at the corners, promptly suppressing the urge to smile.

"It's a family name. Thankfully the only person who calls me that is my mother when I've done something wrong."

Amused, I glanced over my shoulder at my crew.

"Team, go have a break. Mr. Mackenzie and I need to chat."

My kitchen crew promptly headed out to the back courtyard. They'd take a well-deserved break before we set up for evening prep and handed off to the dinner crew.

In the quiet kitchen, Mac and I considered each other as only two people who'd seen each other naked could—intensely.

"Lunch was fucking ace," Mac finally said, breaking the silence between us.

I tapped my lip, trying to peg which order

would have been his. "The Americana burgers, right?"

He nodded.

"Next time, try the lamb. It's really freaking good."

"Noted."

I turned, picking up my knife from the counter and absently reaching for a capsicum to dice.

"Are you still interested in renting me the room?" Mac asked, coming to stand beside me at the counter.

"Depends." I kept chopping, glancing up at him. "Are you gonna make this awkward?"

He tilted his head to one side. "Whatcha mean?"

I shrugged as I expertly shifted the perfectly diced pepper pieces to one side and reached for another capsicum. "You scratched an itch. I'm not the dating or marrying type. I wasn't looking for a relationship, and I'm definitely not looking for a repeat."

He winced. "I was that bad?"

Memories of that night had heat pooling low in my belly. "Not at all. It's just I don't do seconds."

Mac stood quiet for a long moment, the low hum of the machines around us and the rhythmic thump of my knife against the cutting board the only interruptions.

"I'm not gonna lie, Anika, I'm interested in you." He raised his hands in surrender, warding off my protest. "But I can also respect when a woman says no." He dropped his hands. "If you're cool with it, I'll take the room. Not sure how much longer I can live with the nudist sex bunnies."

I chuckled. "Kitchen or hall?"

Mac shuddered. "Kitchen. And on the damned countertop."

I grinned. "Booth six for me. I thought they'd gone home, and we had a raccoon or some shit. I will never unsee that."

He leaned a hip against the counter, crossing his arms over his chest. "So, you see my predicament."

I did, but that didn't mean I was a hundred percent on board with him moving in. You didn't live with someone you'd previously slept with.

Or want to sleep with again.

I bit my lip, chopping the capsicum while considering my options. The only reason I was thinking about taking on a short-term room-mate was to earn a bit of extra cash to pay for this bloody Anniversary holiday. Farrah was going to be in a bind, and I didn't want to dip into my savings account for this.

Parts of the town were still affordable for first-home buyers, and unless I was looking at Millionaire Row (which I could never afford), I wanted to buy within the next two years.

"Alright." I laid down my knife, cleaning my hands on my apron. "But there will be ground rules."

Mac straightened, glancing around. "Should I get a pen and paper for this?"

I hid a smile, shaking my head. "No, they're easy enough to remember." I held up a hand, ticking off the rules on my fingers.

"One, we don't talk about, allude to, or reference our sexual history."

Mac grinned. "Can I think about it in the privacy of my own bedroom?"

I faltered. "You... you think about us?"

"You," he corrected. "It's kind of hard to get someone who tastes like sugar and spice out of my mind."

A little frisson of attraction zinged between us. This man was screwing with my equilibrium.

Pull it together, Anika!

"Warning, I might be sugar and spice, but I'm rarely nice."

He chuckled, his hand going to his shoulder

and rubbing along his collarbone. "Oh, I know. I still have the bite marks to prove it."

I couldn't stop the cat-got-the-cream expression I knew was on my face. "I didn't hear you complaining."

"I'm not." He shifted closer. "I loved it."

A part of me – a large part of me – wanted to drift toward him. I wanted to lay my hand on his chest and kiss him. I wanted to let him lift me onto the counter and fuck me while I bit him again.

Instead, I shook my head, holding up my second finger. "Two, we split the cleaning and cooking – fifty-fifty."

He shrugged. "Seems fair."

"And three, I reserve the right to kick you out of my home at any point for any reason."

Mac held out his hand. "Shall we shake on it?"

I slipped mine into his, my skin sizzling at his touch. I shivered, goosebumps rising on my skin.

"I think we need an addendum," he told me, his voice husky, his eyes flashing.

"And that would be?"

"I reserve the right to try and change your mind... if you keep giving me looks like the one you're wearing now."

My nipples, those traitorous bitches, responded to the gravel in his voice.

"Mac..."

He stepped back, shaking his head. "Sorry, I shouldn't have done that."

Why not?

Ugh, I was one of *those* people – the people who send mixed signals and then get annoyed when the other person has no idea what you want.

Get your shit together, Anika.

Mac blew out a long breath. "When can I move in?"

"Does tomorrow work for you?"

He nodded. "Any specific time?"

"Morning? I can let you in and show you around. I just gotta be done by eleven to get here."

"Works for me."

Mac turned to stroll to the exit, hesitating in the doorway. "Your nickname is Ah-ni, not Ann-ee, isn't it?"

"Ani? Yeah."

He nodded once as if filing that away. "See you tomorrow."

He left me staring at the doors, wondering if I'd just made the biggest mistake of my life.

Fuck you, Kapil. Seriously. Fuck you for forcing me into this situation.

7

Mac

Anika's condo wasn't at all what I expected. I'd envisioned apartments or something similar to a hotel – concrete and glass. Instead, the buildings were interconnected single-story family homes clustered together around a shared, sheltered courtyard. The building itself consisted of weather-beaten redwood cladding, large windows, and thick stone. It looked almost like a barn, but for the unique angles and multitude of windows and balconies.

"This town just keeps on surprising me," I remarked to Gunnar as he put the truck in park.

"Surprised the hell out of me too, when I first came here." He gestured at the building.

"Some architect managed to talk the locals into selling him land for slightly above the asking price so long as he could build whatever he wanted. The locals were cool with it, so long as it met their requirements of being accessible and affordable housing. The architect won a couple of awards, the landowners purchased it back for a decent price, and the renters get a kickass place to live without paying top dollar."

I shook my head. "Seriously, this town."

Gunnar laughed. "I know, right?"

Anika's pad was the last one on the far left, with neighbours only on one side. On the other, she had a clear view out to the national park and down the coast to the marina.

"I can't believe we're only a short walk from the marina," I remarked, pressing her doorbell. "It feels like a world away."

Anika pulled the door open, and I sucked in a breath, once again hit by her effortless beauty. She wore a slouchy sweater that swamped her curves, her legs clad in bright green leggings which hugged her calves and thighs. Her hair was pulled back into a high messy ponytail, and a bandana wrapped around her head.

"Hey." She stepped aside, waving us through. "Come in, come in. I've just finished baking and need some guinea pigs."

She guided us through the condo, pointing

out the various rooms on our way to the main living area. The living, kitchen, and dining rooms looked out over a large deck, taking advantage of the windows to invite the ocean views in.

"Here." Anika sliced two generous pieces of pie, quickly plating them up before handing them to us. "It needs something, but I'm not sure what."

I lifted a forkful of the decadent dessert to my mouth, moaning as the chocolate and cream hit my tongue. A second bite had the chocolate mix with gooey caramel and salty pretzels, the combination exploding in an ecstasy of bliss on my tongue.

"This." Gunnar pointed at his slice. "Doesn't need a goddamned thing. It's fucking perfect." He forked another bite.

Anika rolled her eyes and looked at me, her expression expectant. "Don't let me down. Something's missing, what is it?"

I took another bite, this time pulling the flavours apart and testing it out.

"It's too sweet," I finally said. "It's not missing something so much as it has too much sweetness."

Anika snapped her fingers. "Yes! That's it." She turned back to her kitchen, the counter a mess of bowls and utensils, muttering to herself.

I glanced at Gunnar, who shrugged, bringing another bite to his lips.

"Peanut butter!" Anika declared, holding up a jar. "That's what you need, isn't it, my pie baby?"

She reached for a bowl and a spoon, removing big helpings of peanut butter from the jar.

"Um, am I okay to start moving my shit in?" I asked, placing my now empty plate back on the counter.

"Hundred percent." Anika waved the spoon in our direction. "You want a hand?"

"Nah, I travelled light."

Gunnar and I grabbed my bags from the truck, tossing them into my assigned room. It wasn't large, but I didn't need much. A queen bed, a closet, and the main bathroom down the hall.

And Anika in the next room.

I shoved that thought aside, trying once again to put her back in the friendship/roommate box. It was fucking hard; the woman had blown my mind. She'd been unabashed, beautiful—no—fucking *phenomenal* that night in the hotel.

And the fact she'd brandished a knife without any hesitation? Hot as fuck.

Gunnar yelled goodbye to Anika, heading out. He'd decided to run back into town. Apparently, he needed to 'keep his body pristine' for Ella. I assumed that translated to he'd eaten too many burgers over the last few months.

I put my shit away, listening to Anika bang and mutter her way around the kitchen.

Back home, I was a solitary guy. I'd lived by myself for a few years, not even sharing with a goldfish. I hadn't been lonely – God knew I had enough friends and family to keep me busy. But I found the noise reassuring. It felt... homey. Right.

Having stalled long enough, I headed back to the kitchen. Anika looked up, gesturing me over with an impatient wave.

"Come here." she scooped a spoonful of something thick out of a bowl. "Try this."

I accepted the offered spoon, tasting peanuts, chocolate, and just a hint of salt.

"That is fucking good," I said, licking the spoon clean while gazing longingly at the bowl. "Please, Ma'am, can I have more?"

"No." Anika tapped my hand. "You can have more when the masterpiece is complete."

"I look forward to it." I hesitated, looking at

the mess of bowls and utensils strewn across the bench. "Can I help?"

Anika reached into a bag of flour, sprinkling it across a clean part of the counter. "You could wash up if you want?"

"Sure."

I filled her generous sink with hot, soapy water and began clearing the pile beside the sink. Anika pointed to the equipment she was finished using as she rolled out a cookie crumb base.

"Have you always wanted to be a ship... builder? Sailor? Captain?"

I grinned, flicking suds off my arms as I reached for a large mixing bowl. "Shipwright. And no, not a shipwright, exactly. I just wanted to work with my hands. I like creating things."

Anika paused in her rolling. "I get that. Some people think I just throw things in a pan and hope for the best. But there's an art to food. Creating something that nourishes people means something to me."

I found myself observing her, watching the rhythmic movement of her arms, the stretch and grip of her fingers, and the way her lips pursed slightly as she concentrated on working the crust just right. Anika's movements were utilitarian in nature, but there was a sensuality that she exuded that I found intoxicating.

Pull yourself together, man. The woman said no. Respect her wishes.

I gave myself a mental shake before answering her. "Exactly. I like knowing people will use something I built for years. That they'll have memories of the crafts we build."

She handed me the rolling pin, then shuffled the base, gently lifting it and laying it down into the waiting pie dish.

"Sometimes I think people forget that there's a wealth of history in what they see as a simple job."

I considered her statement as I ran a damp cloth over the wood. "What do you mean?"

She shrugged, pressing the dough into the dish. "I guess I might be a bit biased. My parents are great, they're big believers in doing what you love. But my brother? Not so much."

"What's he do?"

"Stockbroker. He and his wife are...." She huffed out a laugh. "It sounds awful, but they're snobs. Farrah and I –"

"Farrah?"

"My sister. There's only three of us."

I nodded, waiting for her to continue.

"Anyways, Farrah and I don't earn as much as Kapil. I mean, sure, we're awesome. I'm part owner of a successful restaurant. While Farrah runs the town's wildlife preservation. She's also the town mayor, which isn't even a paid job."

"Really? I always thought those kinds of positions were pretty good, finance-wise."

Anika shook her head. "She does it because she loves this town. The preservation pays her a wage, such as it is." Anika poured the peanut butter mixture into the pie crust, handing me the dirty bowl.

"She can be mayor and a public servant?"

Anika laughed. "Hell no. The town refused to fund the preservation back when Farrah was in high school. She found private donors to keep the doors open. Now they do a bunch of different stuff under her watch."

"Such as?"

Anika shrugged. "Last year, they held fundraisers like movies at the beach in summer, a bake sale, that kind of thing. She names some of the animals after famous people and pops them up on social media. Sometimes the famous person hears about it and donates to it as a give-back scheme. Mostly it's their fans who hear about it and get a kick out of it."

"Smart," I said, reaching for the jug she'd just discarded. "You finished with this?"

"Yeah, thanks."

I dipped it in the water, cleaning the chocolate from the glass. "So, you guys are the good ones in the family, and your brother is the soulless corporate vampire?"

She burst out laughing, "I'm gonna use that the next time I'm forced to talk to him."

I grinned, enjoying her laughter.

"Anyways." She shrugged. "It's hard not to feel like a failure for choosing a different path, you know?"

I shook the water off my hands, looking for a dish towel.

"On the oven," Anika said, nodding in that direction as she smoothed the chocolate ganache over the peanut butter mousse.

"I find it hard to think you're a failure when you live in this place." I waved a hand to encompass the room. "You're part owner of a restaurant. You have great friends and a kickass job. Not sure what your so-called brother considers success, but I'd say you're living a damned good definition."

Her spatula paused, her gaze finding mine.

"You're pretty amazing, Ani."

She flushed, breaking our stare to begin smoothing the chocolate once more.

I let her have that escape.

"You said you were working today?"

"Yeah, I got the cover shift – eleven 'til seven."

"You want me to make dinner tonight?" I asked, reaching for the fridge.

"Um, sure. If you want to. No pressure though, I can just grab something at work."

I considered the contents of her fridge.

"You got steak?"

"No. I don't eat cow."

I sent her a surprised look.

"I should say I *try* not to eat cow." She laughed wryly. "My dad's Hindu. I was raised on chicken and lamb." She shrugged. "But occasionally, I slip."

I nodded, readjusting my menu ideas. "Stuffed chicken work for you?"

"Sounds great." She lifted the pie nodding at the fridge. "Can you hold that for a second?"

I held the door while she slid the heavy bowl onto a shelf.

She straightened, shifting slightly to allow me to shut the door.

"Thanks."

I nodded, suddenly realising how close we were. Our bodies nearly touched as we stood, staring at each other.

Fucking move!

"I... I should –"

I nodded, sucking in a breath. "You gotta get to work."

"Yes!" She leapt on that like a lifeline. "I'll see you later."

She disappeared down the hall and into her room, leaving me in a semi-clean kitchen with a raging hard-on.

She said no, I reminded myself silently.

But her eyes and body said yes. Perhaps some rules are meant to be broken...

"Well, fuck."

8

Anika

Mac and I fell into a surprisingly easy rhythm. On days I had lunch service, I cooked. On nights I pulled a mid or late shift, he cooked. We split chores and finances. Our only squabble came over what to watch on the one TV in the house – I'd slowly been converted to survivalist and endurance reality TV while Mac was still on the fence about Bollywood dramas.

As the weeks stretched into a month, I found myself becoming increasingly attracted to the man in my house. I'd expected that with time Mac would annoy me. Instead, I found myself coming home to cooked meals and engaging conversations. He fixed my leaking taps and serviced my bike – things I could do myself but rarely had the time.

Mac, I was discovering, was an exceptional individual, which made the chemistry that hummed between us that much harder to ignore.

"You're free today, right?" Mac asked as he poured himself coffee.

I blinked up at him, my vision still blurry from sleep. "What?"

He grinned, nudging a mug of coffee across the counter toward me. "Drink up."

I automatically followed his direction, muttering, "Yes, sir."

Even in my sleepy state, I caught the flash of heat in his eyes before he looked away, letting out a long, slow breath.

"Today? You're off work?"

I waved a hand at the calendar stuck to the fridge. "If it says so on the holy schedule, then it must be true."

He grinned, "Gunnar's headed up to the Cape to drop Gabby off for her apprenticeship, and Ella mentioned that she was working."

I raised an eyebrow in his direction, "and you're thinking... what?"

"You wanna go out on the water with me?"

I blinked. "As in, on one of your boats?"

"Yeah," he tapped the counter, his fingers

drumming a quick beat. "It's just... it's been too fucking long, and I don't know the area well enough to go out by myself, so I figured I'd ask you."

I knew it had to be bullshit. The man was an experienced sailor. Ella had mentioned that he'd done a solo tour around the world a few years back. And yet, as false as his words were, I couldn't help the liquid warmth that pooled in my belly.

"The last boat I went on was a cruise during high school." I shuddered. "I ate a scoop of shitty potato salad the first night and spent the whole trip worshipping the porcelain throne. Worst food poisoning of my life."

He laughed, his fingers stilling. "If I promise to leave the potato salad at home, will you come?"

A weird fluttering sensation began in my middle, my chest suddenly light and tight at the same time.

"Umm... yeah. If you want."

He grinned. "Oh, I want."

And there it was, that zing of attraction that filled every room we were in. It felt like we were tinder, walking around just waiting for a spark to ignite us.

One and done. Remember?

I reached for my coffee, desperately lifting it to my lips to hide from him.

"Can you be ready in an hour?"

I dropped the cup, narrowing my eyes at him. "An hour?"

His grin widened. "If I make you breakfast first?"

"Oh, buddy, you were always gonna be making me breakfast."

Mac laughed, and the sound did strange things to me. Like hardening my nipples and causing my traitorous thighs to clench.

Stop it!

Mac whipped up toast and eggs while I got dressed, pulling on a light summer dress over my bikini and adding a hat and cardigan.

"What do you think?" I asked, performing a slow twirl in our hall. "Am I good?"

He cleared his throat, his eyes glued to my legs. "Umm... maybe shoes?"

I nodded, kicking off my flip-flops and returning to my room to dig through for some sneakers.

"Bikes or car?" Mac asked, shutting and locking the door behind us.

I glanced at our bags. While he'd made breakfast, I'd whipped up some lunch and snacks, to which he'd added towels and sunscreen.

"Let's take the car. I'll probably be sun drunk by the time we get back."

He drove the short route to the marina, parking in the employee-only spot. The parking lot was full of locals and tourists all out to enjoy the beautiful day.

"You've painted," I commented as we began to stroll down to the boat docks.

"Yeah, Gunnar insisted. Said that if we want our marina to be taken seriously, it needed to look professional."

I nodded, approving of the white and navy-blue colour scheme. The marina had been run down, and tired-looking after the old owner ran into some financial trouble. Gunnar taking it over was a massive financial outlay, but I could already see the potential. All around us, people were stopping to look at the progress of the repairs or sit and enjoy the sun on the new benches they'd installed.

"Impressive work for only a few months."

"Well, when you're motivated and throw enough money at the problem...."

I didn't doubt this was costing the Larssons a pretty penny, but I'd seen Mac coming home. He often returned sweaty and exhausted, covered in all manner of paint, grime or dust. More than once, he'd fallen asleep beside me on the couch, his gentle snores somehow amusing and comforting at the same time.

"I'm over here." He led me to a small yacht named *Valkyrie*.

"This is Gunnar's boat, isn't it?" I asked, taking his hand as he helped me step across the void and onto the deck.

"Whatever gave that away?"

We both chuckled.

"The man is obsessed with my best friend."

He nodded, unlocking the hatch. "Yeah, I'm glad. He deserves happiness."

I lifted my eyebrows in surprise, but he missed it, instead focusing on swinging the hatch open, hitching it then gesturing me down the stairs into the galley.

In the belly of the boat was a small kitchen with a small dining area, a teeny-tiny bathroom, and a bedroom with a double bed behind one of the doors. It was more than enough for two people.

"Here." He pulled a lifejacket from under a seat. "Safety first."

I made a face. "I can swim, you know."

"Yeah, but can you if you've been knocked unconscious by a boom?"

I took it, noting he was also donning one. They weren't overly bulky, but it still felt weird to wear.

"Let's get out of the harbour then I'll teach you how to steer this baby."

He showed me the ropes (literally) and then got us moving, occasionally shouting directions as he motored us out of the cluttered harbour and into the open water.

"Where are we going?" I asked, brushing my hair away from my face and readjusting my sunglasses.

"I thought we'd head out to Blossom Island. There's a sheltered cove out there that's reportedly gorgeous."

I loved the way he said gorgeous as if it were a caress. Watching Mac had fast become one of my favourite past times. He looked like a grizzly sea captain or a hairy pirate missing only a parrot. His joy was contagious, infecting me as he pointed out different parts of the boat, explaining what it did and how it worked.

"Your turn." He patted the wheel and then moved a little, making space for me to grip the cool metal.

"Is it just like a car?"

"A little." He settled his hands on my hips, shifting me slightly. "There, you need to be solid and centred, or she can tip you over."

My skin tingled long after he'd removed his hands.

"Now, I'm gonna turn the motor off and get that mainsail up."

Mac fussed around the boat, playing with ropes and lines, clicking things and calling for me to reposition the boat slightly to face into the wind.

After a second, he began to pull a rope, lifting the sail up the mast. When it got close to the top, he fed the rope into a winch, tightening the sail until it looked like a wing.

"That was... impressive."

He grinned, turning the motor off. "Now to raise the jib, and we can get you moving."

The jib turned out to be the front sail, and after a minute the wind caught, and we began to move.

"Woo!" I yelled, laughing as the wind began to lift us and the yacht caught some speed. "This is amazing!"

"Good job." Mac came up, his sunglasses back in place, a hat resting low on his head. "You got her?"

I nodded.

"You can take her in different directions, straight is good, but Blossom Island is," he shifted a little, turning me slightly to face the island. "That way."

I laughed, delighted by both his touch and my newfound boat-driving skill.

"I'm pretty good at driving this thing."

He groaned, dropping his head to my shoulder and giving me a little shake. "Driving? Really Anika?"

"Well, give me the words then."

"Sailing. Or steering. Occasionally people use piloting, but that's not a term I'd use."

"Noted." I gave a vicious jerk to the steering wheel, then frowned as the boat slowed, the sails flapping uselessly.

"Wait, what happened? I was being awesome!"

He laughed. "You lost lift."

"Huh?"

"Lift, it's a matter of physics. Velocity, pressure, and force."

I waved a hand. "Don't. I can't deal with math today. Give me the footnotes."

"The wind hits the sails and the keel, the fins that sit under the boat then acts as a counterbalance to the wind to push the boat forward." He licked his finger and lifted it into the air as if feeling for the wind.

"In other words, I turned the wrong way?"

"Precisely."

Gods, if that isn't the story of my life, I don't know what is.

We sailed for a little while, chatting about

boating, my work, and the weather. It felt both normal and somehow momentous.

I didn't do this with men I'd slept with. I didn't have this casual friendship or enjoy their company. I couldn't. I'd get attached, and they'd inevitably break my heart. I'd developed three rules to protect myself;

1. Keep things casual
2. Leave first
3. Never follow up

Nothing about today felt casual.

Just keep it light. Don't let things stray.

We drew closer to Blossom Island while Mac consulted his map.

"There's anchorage around that point," he said, nodding at the outcropping. "That's where we're headed."

We dropped anchor in the small cove, the water beautiful and still, thanks to the shelter provided by the crescent-shaped cove.

"This is gorgeous," I said once he'd given me the okay that everything was secure.

"You haven't been here?"

I shook my head. "No, I think the cruise turned me off boating for a few years."

"Well, you've obviously been missing out."

"Hundred percent," I agreed, sighing once

again at the stunning water and picturesque private beach.

"Lunch?"

"Sounds good."

Mac set up a small rug on the deck, the sail providing partial shade. Between us, I laid out sandwiches and soda, with brownies and Tupperware cups filled with a mix of berries for dessert.

"I could get used to this," Mac muttered around a bite of his Reuben sandwich. "Though I thought you didn't eat cow?"

"I don't. I'm having chicken. But Gunnar mentioned a Rueben was your favourite so I brought some meat home for you." I caught his stare. "What?"

He shook his head. "Nothing... just... thanks."

I shrugged, feeling strangely uncomfortable. "It's not a big deal, Mac."

We ate in silence for a few minutes, watching the water.

I breathed out a sigh, relaxing under the warm sun. "This is beautiful. Any time you wanna take me out for a sail, I'm in."

"I'll be sure to do it more often."

We chatted about the marina and the progress of the workshop. After clearing it out, the contractors had started last week, which meant Gunnar and Mac were now splitting their days between a hired workshop to do some small boat-building tasks and supporting updates and repairs to the marina.

Mac cleaned up, telling me to stay while he checked the boat over.

I did as he directed, stretching out on the rug, my body enjoying the sun and the gentle rocking under us. I woke an hour later to Mac reading a book beside me.

"Hey, sleeping beauty." His lips curled into a smile, his eyes lighting. "Better?"

"Wonderful," I admitted feeling surprisingly rested. "Sorry about that."

He shrugged. "You wanna head back or go for a swim or...?"

I shifted, grimacing at the sweat that soaked my back. "A swim sounds great."

He marked his place in his book, dog-earring the corner of a page, then set it aside as he stood. I was about to follow but froze as his hands went to the bottom of his shirt, pulling it off and tossing it away.

Oh, MacDaddy.

Hefty. Heavy. Weighty. Girthy. These were the words that sprang to mind as I stared at Mac's chest. He was a mountain of a man, and I suddenly found an interest in climbing.

Stop it! Temporary, remember?

No matter how I tried to convince myself otherwise, I wanted him. Desperately.

"You coming?"

I whipped my dress over my head, throwing it away. Mac had seen me without clothes, but the way his gaze caressed my body felt almost... wicked.

"Last one to shore has to buy dinner," I yelled, running for the side of the yacht. With a quick, one-two step, I cannonballed off the side, landing with a giant splash in the water. The water enveloped me, cooling the heat of my skin.

Too bad it can't cool my raging attraction.

I kicked to the surface, striking out for the shore. It wasn't too far. Mac fell in beside me, easily keeping pace.

Damned man.

As we got closer, we picked up the pace, both of us trying to outdo the other. As we hit the shallows, beginning to dash through the water, a wave of inspiration struck.

Bad, Anika!

Mac overtook me, his long legs quickly eating up the beach.

"Mac!" I called, briefly pausing to whip my bikini top off. Only his head twisted, a teasing grin on his face until he caught sight of my bare chest. Shock had him tripping and falling, crashing into the shallow water.

Laughing, I ran past, one hand clamped over my small tits to keep them from bouncing too much, the other throwing my wet top at him as I passed.

"Foul!" he cried, catching the top and struggling to stand. "Cheating!"

"This is the Thunderdome, baby! No rules."

I sprinted for the shore, Mac crashing behind me. My feet were mere steps from clearing the water and hitting the dry sand when an arm clamped around my middle, lifting me up and swinging me around.

I squealed, kicking to be let down. Instead, Mac backed up, crossing our imaginary line first.

"No fair!" I cried, wiggling in his arms. "You can't manhandle a combatant."

"Oh, so now there are rules?"

I laughed, still struggling. Mac tripped and fell backward, bearing the weight of me on him with an *oof*.

"Oh shit." I twisted, pressing a hand to the sand beside us and staring down at him. "You okay?"

His eyes were closed, a pained look on his face. "I will be."

"Where does it hurt?" I asked, pushing back and running hands over his chest. "Here?"

He shook his head. "Just my cock."

"Your cock? What have you done to—oh." I bit my lip, looking appreciatively at the impressive hard-on tenting his swimming shorts. "I see."

He chuckled, eyes still closed. "Anika, do me a favour?"

"Anything."

"Put your top on." He held the garment up, waiting for me to take it. "I'm only human, babe."

I realised this was a crossroads moment. I could take the top, put it on, and we'd quietly try to stuff each other back in the friendship box.

Or you could be naughty.

Gods, the temptation was overpowering.

"Mac?"

"What?" he asked, still holding out the top.

"You said this is a private beach, yeah?"

"Uh-huh. Why?"

I reached for the ties at my hip that kept my bikini bottoms together.

"Just checking." I tugged at the tie, letting the bottoms fall free. "Mac?"

"Can you just take the damned top?" he asked, his voice strained.

"No, I think you should open your eyes first."

He did, blinking and inhaling a sharp breath. "Christ almighty."

I grinned, running my hands up my body to cup my breasts, offering them to him. "Like what you see?"

"Please, Gods, Anika. You need to be sure."

I bit my lip, running my thumbs over my sensitive nipples. "Oh, I am. Friends with benefits?"

He froze for a second, his eyes glued to my hands. With effort, I saw him look up, meeting my gaze.

"No. We do this, I want the girlfriend experience."

My hands froze. "What?"

"You heard me." He pushed up off the sand, his cock rigid and heavy as it bounced with his movement. "I want snuggling and laughter, fucking amazing sex and dates." He leaned in until his lips were a mere breath from mine. "I want to be wooed, Ani."

A strangled giggle worked its way up my throat. "I'm sorry, what?"

"Wined and dined. I was so stunned by your appearance that night at the bar I forgot to add those caveats. This time I'm doing it right."

I giggled, but nerves fought with fear, goose-bumps rising on my skin.

Don't do it.

"Can't we keep this casual?" There was a thread of desperation in my voice.

Slowly Mac shook his head, water droplets falling from his hair to land like diamonds on his shoulders. "I can't do casual with you."

My heart seized, but no words came out.

For a moment, Mac stared at me, disappointment carving itself into his skin. He reached forward, cupping my cheek.

"It's okay, Ani. I understand. I'm not the kind of guy you want."

Without thinking, I reached out, wrapping my arms around him and boosting myself up to press against him, my lips meeting his.

He kissed me immediately, his arms wrapping around my body, his mouth hot and wet and oh so possessive.

"Yes?" he asked, his breathing harsh.

"Yes," I answered, taking a leap of faith.

His mouth found mine again, his tongue plundering. We kiss and kiss, our hands running over sun-warmed skin, his body grinding against mine.

More.

I push him down, straddling his hips.

"Anika, we can't—"

I silenced his protest with a kiss, grinding myself on him. He groaned, his hands skimming the side of my body to come up and cup my breasts.

"Fucking love your tits," he grunted against my lips. "Gonna paint these pretty breasts with my cum."

Yes.

My hips picked up pace, my body desperate for release. I rode Mac's cock through his shorts, the wet material both pleasurable and abrasive. The dichotomy of that, coupled with the heat of our bodies, of the sun and sand, and the cool breeze, resulted in sensation overload.

I lost all sense of control. All power over my orgasm. I came, my head thrown back, a satisfied cry catching on the wind.

"Fuck yes." Mac surged up, his hips pumping as he dragged his cock along the sensitive flesh of my pussy, pumping until he came.

He fell back onto the sand, bringing me down with him. I lay on his body, desperately sucking in air, both horrified and aroused by what we had just done.

"Well," Mac coughed, his hands gliding over my skin. "At least we used protection."

I huffed out a laugh. "Oh yes, swim shorts are recommended by two out of three gynaecologists."

He fisted my hair, bringing my mouth to his. "Smartass."

Mac kissed me as if we hadn't just dry-humped to completion on a deserted beach. He kissed me as if he hungered for me, as if I were his first, his last, his only meal.

"Did you bring condoms?" I asked, panting when we finally broke apart.

"I think I might have one or two back on the boat."

I groaned, thudding my head against his chest. "You're really gonna make me swim all that way to get some nookie?"

He chuckled, his chest shaking me. "Well, I wasn't exactly expecting you to jump me."

I shrugged. "Complaining?"

"Fuck no." Mac rolled me, taking me to the sand, his big body pressing into me as he kissed me senseless.

9

Anika

Days later, I was still thinking about that day on the beach... and the subsequent sex fest we'd indulged in upon returning to the boat. I swear I was still finding sand in places sand had no right to be.

I'd never felt this kind of crazy pull before. The attraction and the need to claim Mac.

I was normally a hit-it-and-quit-it kind of girl – here for a good time, not a long time. I'd tried the boyfriend thing in school, then culinary college. Two had cheated on me, the third hadn't wanted to commit. They'd all said the same thing – I was the girl you fucked, not the kind you took home to momma.

Lesson learned. I'd buried any dreams of

picket fences and wedding sarees, contenting myself with the occasional one-night lover.

But Mac? He was the first man in years that cut through. He was the first guy I'd let in. And to complicate matters, he was living in my house. This situation was fast turning into the very definition of a hot mess.

We had sex every night. And sometimes in the morning as well. While we were keeping it quiet, we didn't seem to have any control when it came to each other. Mac made me wish for things I had no business desiring.

And that alone was terrifying.

"Ani, we're pretty quiet. Did you wanna head out?" My sous chef, Sam, asked. I glanced at the clock, seeing it was a quarter to seven. I was meant to be staying 'till eight, but with a slow dining night, the extra hour at home with Mac would be welcome.

Who even are you?

I lifted a scoop. "Let me get this ice cream in the chiller, then I'll finish up."

Sam nodded, turning back to the pass to slide plates of freshly cooked fish up for the hovering waiter.

I pulled the freshly churned ice cream from the machine, dipping my spoon in to have a taste. Delicious vanilla exploded on my tongue, the taste intense and comforting.

Most people thought vanilla was boring with no pizazz. But I knew the truth, when done well, vanilla was the most complex of flavours.

"Good?" Jack asked, watching me with a grin.

I nodded. "Perfect."

I scooped the ice cream free from the churner into a container, sealing it to ensure there would be no ice crystals, and then popped it in the freezer. That done, I discarded my apron, calling goodbye to my staff.

I paused in the breakroom, checking our schedule.

We did rotational weeks, making sure everyone got a weekend off, and no one pulled the late shifts too often. Burnout was an issue in our industry, and I wanted my staff to be fighting fit when they came to work. If you didn't love your job, it showed on the plate. And average food was never acceptable.

I wouldn't have another weekend off to spend with Mac for at least two weeks.

Damn.

I headed for the back office, finding Ella doing the numbers.

"I'm about to head home," I told her, leaning against the door jamb. "It's quiet for a Sunday. The kitchen might let Jack go early too."

She nodded, leaning back in her chair and

rubbing her eyes. "It's coming up to finals at school. I expect most of the families are trying to get their kids to cram." She spread her hands, encompassing the printed sheets of numbers spread across her desk. "And if my numbers are correct —"

"Which they always are," I said, poking my tongue out at her.

She grinned. "Then we'll have doubled our profit from this time last year."

I let out a low whistle. "That's massive, Ella."

She nodded, her cheeks flushing with plea-sure. "We're doing it, Ani. Everyone bet against us, but we're doing it."

I held up my hand, and she air-high-fived me from across the room, both of us grinning.

"You headed home?"

I nodded, then paused. "Can I ask you something?"

"Shoot."

"With Gunnar, shit between you got real quite quickly." I cleared my throat. "How did you know?"

She blinked, tilting her head to one side. "Know what?"

I shrugged, trying for casual. "You know... that he was 'the one'." I made air quotes with my fingers. "What made him different?"

Instead of laughing me off or offering a bullshit answer, Ella leaned back in her chair, tilting her head back to stare at the ceiling as she considered my question.

"I guess some part of me knew when he walked in. There was... this indescribable connection between us. It was like my soul knew." She blew out a breath. "But I'm an overly logical creature, so as much as I wanted to believe in love, I knew that there was a chance things wouldn't work out."

"How did you get over that?"

Ella shrugged, "I had to have faith that I was enough. And if Gunnar had left me for whatever reason, then I needed to know I would be able to live without him." She leaned forward, resting her arms on her desk. "You don't choose a relationship to stay the same. You choose to trust that other person to grow with you. If Gunnar left me tomorrow, I would be devastated—like mainlining ice cream and swearing off love ruined." She chuckled. "But I'd survive. Because I know I'm more than just Gunnar's woman. I'm a badass, and I'm deserving of a lifetime of love."

I nodded, swallowing. "I'm really glad you found a guy that looks at you like you hung the moon."

Ella flapped a hand at me. "That's not all

that I get to hang, if you catch my drift." She wiggled her eyebrows suggestively.

"First, ew, overshare. Second, happy for you because, yes, to good dick. And third, what are we working with here?" I pushed off the door jamb, holding my hands out about six inches apart and widening them. "Tell me when to stop."

She threw a pencil at me, which I caught, tucking it into my bun. "Go home!"

"Yes, boss." I snapped her a smart salute but hesitated in the doorway.

"Ella?"

"Mm?"

"Thanks."

"For?"

I shrugged. "Everything?"

She huffed out a laugh, waving me off. "Go get some sleep, you sappy Chef. I'll see you Tuesday."

I turned to leave.

"And Ani?"

I glanced over my shoulder. "Yeah?"

"Tell Mac I said hi."

I chuckled, appreciating the fact I had such a perceptive friend. "Will do."

I mulled over her words as I rode home, the wind a little brisk but the night clear and beautiful.

I had to have faith that I was enough.

And that was my problem. I'd never been enough for anyone, let alone myself.

I blew out a deep breath, tilting my head to the night sky, but mother moon held no answers for me tonight.

Outside my townhouse, I pulled out my phone, fingers hovering over the keyboard.

HOT CHEF

Hey, I got off early.

MACDADDY

Thank the Gods. I'm dying to watch the next episode. Do you have any idea how hard it's been not to cheat?

I grinned, fingers flying as I typed out a response.

HOT CHEF

I hear in some circles pleasure denial is a kink.

MACDADDY

Tell you what, we'll give that a go in bed later. I bet you couldn't last five minutes.

Likely true.

HOT CHEF

Can I admit something?

MACDADDY

Any time. Particularly if it's
naughty ;)

I gulped, my palms suddenly sweaty.

HOT CHEF

Sometimes you scare me.

His response was surprisingly quick, my phone vibrating in less than 30 seconds with his incoming call. I stared at the phone, biting my lip as I swiped to accept.

"Hey," I whispered, my heart beating through my chest. "Good night?"

"I don't know, maybe. It depends on why I scare you."

I sucked in a breath, his warm, rough voice calming my tension. "I'm not a relationship kind of girl, Mac. I'm not the girl you take home to momma. But..."

"But?" he prompted when I didn't continue.

"But I'd like to try. With you."

"Thank Christ." I heard movement on his end of the line.

"Where are you?"

I chuckled nervously. "Outside."

The door opened, and I saw him standing in

the doorway, backlit by the light coming from inside our house.

"You gonna come in?" he asked into the phone as if knowing how much I needed him to continue pretending that there was distance between us.

"Yeah, but...." I swallowed. "I think I like you, Mac. And that is bloody terrifying."

I saw his teeth flash as he grinned. "I *know* I like you. And it's fucking amazing."

I chuckled, nerves sending the butterflies fluttering in my belly. "I've been hurt before. It sucked. I don't know how to do the relationship thing."

"Then we'll work it out together." He stepped back, holding the door open. "Come home, Anika. Your boyfriend wants to kiss you."

I hung up the phone, taking a deep breath. This was it. This was the moment I stood at a crossroads and made my choice.

And knowing that, knowing this was a terrifying moment, I put one foot in front of the other until I'd made my way to Mac.

He closed the door behind me and stood in the hall, hands held loosely by his side. He didn't make a move to approach me.

I shifted from foot to foot. "Are you just gonna stand there?"

"Yeah, you need to make the first move this

10

Mac

I viciously drove another nail into the new wood, trying to work out the simmering frustration in my blood.

Ani was withdrawing.

The night she'd chosen to step toward me ad been a game-changer. I'd already started lking with Gunnar about the possibility of me wing to the Cove permanently – to say the was thrilled was an understatement. He'd ically offered me shares in the marina.

'd asked what had changed my mind, but reluctant to bring up Ani. First, be- had yet to publicly claim me, and sec- there was a part of me that felt she was still unsure about us.

Oh, don't get me wrong, the sex was brilliant. But it was the other stuff she struggled with. Me making her dinner, talking about our day, and snuggling on the couch. Ani always acted as if I were about to stab her in the back and take off with her secret recipes.

It was infuriatingly frustrating.

I took out my simmering tension on another nail, grunting when the hammer drove it home.

"Whoa, boy. What's gotten into you?"

I looked up to see Gunnar approaching, a bag from the Bronze Horseman in his hand.

"That lunch?" I asked, ignoring his question.

"Yep." He shook the bag gently. "But you don't get any until you tell old Gunnar what's crawled up your ass."

I blew out a breath, tossing my hammer into my toolbox, running my hands through my hair. "You don't want to know."

"Bullshit." He sat on one of the new bench seats we'd installed earlier that week, placing the bag down and rummaging inside. "I got a sandwich and soda with your name on it."

I took the offerings, sitting beside him, watching the water as it shimmered and danced.

We chewed in companionable silence for a few minutes before I finally blew out a long sigh. "It's Ani."

"I figured. You slept with her?"

I nodded, looking down at the sandwich I knew she'd made for me. "She's... tricky."

"Tricky how?"

I shrugged. "Just locked up. Suspicious. She acts like me buying her flowers or only wanting to snuggle is this completely foreign concept, and I have some kind of ulterior motive."

"Is it a trust issue?"

I took a bite of the sandwich, chewing slowly as I considered his question. "No. It's more like she doesn't trust herself."

Gunnar blew out a breath. "Ouch."

"Yeah."

We ate in silence for a few moments, the quiet broken only by the waves gently hitting the pylons under our feet and the cry of seagulls as they circled overhead.

"What are you gonna do?" Gunnar finally asked, crushing up his paper wrapper and tossing it in the brown bag.

I sighed. "No idea. I guess keep supporting her as she works through whatever's screwed up her head."

"You want me to chat with Ella? See if she can help?"

"Nah. That feels like a violation of Ani's trust."

He nodded. "Gotcha." Gunnar stood,

clamping a hand on my shoulder. "You'll let me know if you need anything?"

"Of course."

"Good." He squeezed my shoulder. "Now, let's get back to work. And this time? Try not to crush the nails."

As he left, my phone buzzed with a message from Ani.

HOT CHEF

Missed you at lunch. Hope the sandwich was good

I rubbed a hand over my chest, trying to stop the ache.

MACDADDY

Missed seeing you too, but Gunnar wanted a chat. Sandwich was fucking amazing – as always. Did you need something?

Three dots appeared at the bottom of the screen for an excruciatingly long time.

HOT CHEF

I have a favour to ask...

MACDADDY

I already promised to do that thing with my tongue again ;)

HOT CHEF

Ha! Yes, please, and what time?
But that's not what I wanted to
ask... are you free Friday night?

MACDADDY

My only plans are you.

HOT CHEF

Okay well... It's my parents'
anniversary dinner Friday night,
and I wondered if you wanted to
come? No pressure though.
Totally fine to say no!

That ache in my chest eased. I knew the
courage this request would have taken.

MACDADDY

You want me there, I'm there.

HOT CHEF

Thanks. Fair warning, I haven't
brought a guy home since... well,
it's been a while. They'll likely be
curious. It might turn into an
interrogation.

MACDADDY

I'll make sure I have a printout of
my last three tax returns and my
current bank statement. Should I
contact Gunnar for a signed
reference or...?

HOT CHEF

Haha! But seriously, maybe put
Gunnar on notice. Dad might
want to call him.

I chuckled, feeling lighter than I had in over
a week.

MACDADDY

You still going wedding dress
hunting on Saturday?

HOT CHEF

Yeah. Ella's in-laws are down
again. I expect we'll be late.

I blew out a breath, disappointed I wouldn't
be spending her free weekend taking her sailing.

MACDADDY

Keep some time free for me on
Sunday?

HOT CHEF

Always ;)

I tucked my phone back in my pocket,
staring out at the calm waters.

"I'm gonna marry her." The declaration settled in my soul, feeling just right. "Now I just
have to convince Anika."

11

Mac

Ani sat beside me in the cab of my truck. Her hair was down but gently curled. Her makeup was dialled to stunning, and the dress she wore clung to her in all the right ways – I couldn't wait to rip it off.

She twisted her fingers in her lap, fidgeting.

"Hey." I captured her hands in mine. "Just breathe, okay?"

She chuckled. "You wouldn't be saying that if you knew what a big deal this is."

I shot her a look. "Babe, I get it. These are your parents, I'm not gonna whip my cock out and throw it down on the dinner table. Hell, I'll even sit at the table instead of eating off the floor like I normally do."

Her lips tilted up into a reluctant smile. "Don't worry, I brought your bowls in case you change your mind."

I grinned, squeezing her hand before dropping it to regrip the steering wheel to turn into the parking lot at the Bronze Horseman. "Do you think your brother has arrived?"

She groaned. "Of course, he'd do this."

The limo sat in the lot, taking up three spots.

I pulled into a vacant spot toward the back, quickly running around to hold Ani's door open for her.

"Just remember," she said, linking her arm with mine as we strolled toward the entrance. "We all hate Kapil, so it's completely okay to tune him out. Farrah and I have been doing it all our life."

Chuckling, I pulled open the heavy door of the bar, guiding Ani in with a gentle hand to her lower back.

"Hey, Ani," the waitress gave her a small wave. "Your family just arrived."

"I saw," she muttered, straightening her shoulders with a sigh. "Take us to our death."

The waitress giggled, leading us through the main dining area to a private room at the back.

"Here we go." She slid the door open a little,

permitting us entrance. "I'll be back in a minute to get your drink orders."

"Thanks, Jane."

Ani's hand found mine as we stepped into the room.

Seated at the table were five people – Anika's parents, a man and woman who I assumed were Kapil and Anika's sister-in-law Chavvi, and her younger sister, Farrah.

"Hi fam," Anika called, brazening it out. "Happy Anniversary, parents!"

There was a brief pause as they looked from Ani to me and then down to our joined hands.

"Anika!" Her mother rose from the table. "Introduce us?"

I squeezed her hand as she nodded, a flush darkening her cheeks.

"Everyone, this is Mac. Mac, this is my mom, Livia, and my dad, Dev."

I reached out, shaking Dev's hand warmly. "Hi, congratulations. Forty years is a massive achievement."

"Thank you." Dev let my hand go, wrapping his arm around his wife. "Glad you could join us, Mac."

"And this is my sister, Farrah."

I reached out, shaking her hand. "Ms. Mayor, how are you this evening?"

She laughed, her eyes sparkling. "Oh, much, *much* better now."

"And this is my brother, Kapil, and his wife, Chavvi."

Kapil shook my hand, but it was limp and weak. Chavvi was only slightly better.

"Pleasure," I told them, already unimpressed.

"Well, sit," Livia flapped her hands at us. "Sit and tell us all about yourself."

Jane returned, taking drink orders then disappearing.

"Are we not getting menus?" Kapil asked as we settled at the table.

"No, I planned a select menu," Anika answered, shooting me a grin. "I might have even included something special for dessert."

"I'd have preferred to order," Kapil replied, flicking open his napkin and laying it across his lap.

Anika's lips pressed together, a little crinkle wrinkling her brow.

"Well, I can't wait," I said to the table, leaning over to press a kiss to Ani's cheek. "My girl certainly knows how to cook."

I pulled back, catching Dev and Livia exchanging a smile.

The chit-chat was light, mostly focusing on embarrassing family stories, updates about work or friends, and the occasional interrogation. Overall, it was an entirely pleasant evening —except for Kapil and Chavvi.

"You guys ready for dessert?" Jane asked as she cleared our plates.

We'd already had four courses, an appetiser of scallops and fresh oysters, and an entrée that I couldn't even begin to describe beyond it being the lightest and best ceviche I'd ever had in my life. The first course had been a delicious backstrap of lamb, the second a confit yellowfin tuna with wild mushrooms, potato crisps, and preserved peas in' a flavoursome broth.

"Give us a half-hour, thanks Jane," Anika answered, shifting to lean slightly into me.

Kapil raised his glass, taking a sip of his wine. "You know, Ani, that wasn't bad. I'd have added a little more salt to the tuna and used a fresher fish, but it was satisfactory."

This is your first night with her family don't fuck this up by stabbing her brother with your dessert fork.

As if she could hear my thoughts, Ani rested a hand on my leg, giving me a little squeeze.

"Thanks, bro," she said sweetly. "I'll keep that in mind."

"I think it's gift time." Chavvi reached into her small clutch, pulling an envelope free. She handed it to Kapil, who presented it to their parents.

"Chavvi and I got you a little something," he said, pressing a kiss to their mother's cheek.

"And Ani and I contributed," Farrah said after a beat.

"Oh, you guys," Livia looked around the table with a large smile. "You know that tonight was all we wanted."

She ran a finger through the envelope, pulling out a card. She opened it and blinked, her hand flying to her mouth to cover a gasp. "Oh!"

Dev leaned over, reading over her shoulder. "Kids, you really shouldn't have."

I pressed my lips to Ani's ear. "What did you get them?"

"Cruise tickets. Kapil bought them without consulting us. Farrah and I have had to hustle to pay him back."

I rolled my eyes, somehow not surprised. I'd only known the guy for a few hours and already didn't like him.

While Livia and Dev poured over the cruise tickets, effusive in their thanks, Jane returned with a dessert tray.

"What on earth?" I asked, blinking as she placed the tiered tray in the middle of the table.

"Enjoy!"

"Ani... this is..." Livia shook her head. "You always know how to delight us."

"Farrah helped," Ani said, leaning forward to hand out small plates. "We just thought we'd try and recreate some of your favourite dishes from your years together."

I tried bite-size pavlova, delicate chocolate mousse, lamingtons, sticky rice and a rose-flavoured Gulab jamun. Each bite was more delicious than the last – made even more so by the mutinous expressions on Kapil and Chavvi's faces.

No one fucks with my girl.

After dessert and coffee, the table broke up, Kapil and Chavvi escorting Livia and Dev in the limo, Farrah waving goodbye as she got in her small car.

"Home?" I asked Ani, enjoying her weight as she leaned against me.

"Mm, please."

I drove us through the quiet streets, loving the glimpses of moonlight dancing across the water as we headed up to her house.

Inside, I stripped her naked, kissing every inch of bare skin as I slid her dress from her body.

Moonlight flooded through the window, bathing her bedroom in subtle light. That was where I worshipped my girl. Under the watchful gaze of the moon, while she panted and gasped, I tripped over the edge, knowing I was lost to her.

"I love you," I whispered to her as I slid home, her pussy tight around my thick length. "I love you so fucking much, Ani."

Tears glistened on her eyelashes as she blinked up at me.

"You don't need to say anything," I told her, brushing hair from her cheeks. "I just needed you to know."

And with that, I picked up a rhythm designed to drive us both mad with desire. Our bodies moved together, our breathing frantic as she came, clenching and gasping under me.

In the aftermath, she curled into me, silent but content.

I pressed a kiss to her hair, knowing she was overwhelmed and so fucking proud of her for fighting through the fear and sticking with me.

I'm gonna marry this girl.

It was the last thought I had before succumbing to sleep.

12

Anika

"After you," I told Ella, holding the door of the bridal shop open and giving her a little bow with a flourish of my hand.

She giggled, her cheeks pink and eyes sparkling as we entered the store. Accompanying us on this most sacred of missions were Ella's mom, Monique; her gran; Gunnar's sister, Liv; Gunnar's mother, Jemma; and Gunnar's grandmother.

Summer was well underway in Capricorn Cove, the day sticky with the kind of humid heat that precedes a good thunderstorm. Inside, the store was cool and quiet. An instrumental version of an Ed Sheeran song played quietly in the background while two sales assistants served some customers.

Already waiting inside were our friends Honey, Blue, and Collins—all of them holding champagne glasses and wearing wide grins. The only person missing from this oestrogen fest was Gunnar's youngest sister, Astrid, who was busy studying for her finals.

"You're here!" Honey handed her a flute glass. "You're getting married! You're getting married!"

A chubby blonde with a big heart, if I had to describe Honey as a meal, she'd absolutely be a cupcake—delicious, joyful and always sweet.

Collins', a yoga instructor and physical therapist who worked at Honey's health clinic, rich emerald green gaze sparkled as she lifted her glass.

"A toast to the bride." She flicked a long chunk of her thick dark hair over her shoulder, a teasing smile tugging at her lips. "May you find the perfect dress—one that makes your fiancé want to rip it off you."

Laughing, we clinked glasses, even as Ella blushed and Gunnar's mum pretended not to notice.

A woman approached, a large, welcoming smile on her face. "I think that's my cue. For those I have yet to meet, I'm Yasmin and wel-come to Bloom. I'll be assisting you today."

The chirpy young woman wasn't at all what you'd expect from a wedding dress shop as-sistant. I'd known Yasmin for years, and unlike the prim and proper *Say Yes to the Dress* staff you saw on TV who wore demur clothing and acted like judgmental aunts, Yasmin was a god-damned ray of sunshine. For one, she rarely wore anything but the brightest of colours—like the bright yellow sundress that currently encased her curves. For another, her dark hair remained unbound and frizzy-wild thanks to the humidity, her face constantly encased in smiles.

The store felt more like a hipster bar than a dress boutique – despite the numerous racks of wedding, formal, and bridesmaid dresses. The side and back walls were raw brick, the dresses hung from black iron bars. The front of the store was floor-to-ceiling glass, with a bright pink door in between. The window display on one side was a wedding dress – boho chic. While on the other was a mother-of-the-bride display – an amazing salted caramel pantsuit that had me frothing.

No frumpy seconds here.

As the only formal wear store in town, Bloom did a roaring business year-round.

"This is the main store, but I have a special bridal boutique out back. If you'll follow me?"

She led us through a door into a wonderland of frills, lace, and five billion shades of white.

"Now, we have gowns arranged by shade then style. If you find one in a particular style but hate the colour, we can see if it can be ordered. Otherwise, I'm a qualified seamstress and can assist." She gestured at the gowns. "Have a browse, everyone choose some options, and I'll pop them in the dressing room for Ella to try." She hit a button on the wall, opening up the shades over the skylight.

"I find natural light gives a better feel," she explained. "I'll be right back with some finger food and drinks."

"Wait, we get to *eat*?" Liv asked, flicking a hand to push back her curtain of shiny blonde hair.

"You guys do. I just get to be the entertainment," Ella laughed, pulling a dress free.

"This place is seriously lush." Blue ran a hand over the dresses on display. She lifted a dress out, holding it in front of her. "What do you think? It'd suit me, right?"

With her tawny skin and dark colouring, the champagne wedding dress complemented her perfectly.

"Absolutely, you could pull it off," Liv agrees, reaching for a dress. "I'm totally coming back here when I'm engaged."

"When?" Jemma asked, raising an eyebrow. "Is there something you've failed to tell your parents?"

Liv waved dismissively. "I'm a catch. We know it's only a matter of time before someone tries to lock me down."

"Locking you down isn't the issue. It's that you're too picky," Gunnar's grandmother complained. "Just pick one. You can train him after you get the ring."

I snickered, hiding my amusement in a perusal of the dresses.

Ella fell in beside me. "I feel I've made a huge mistake bringing this lot."

"If nothing else, it'll be a killer story."

We grinned, bumping hips.

Yasmin returned with mimosas, water, soda, and a selection of finger sandwiches and tiny tarts. Armed with a selection of fifteen dresses, Ella disappeared into the giant dressing room that took up one full wall while the rest of us lounged around on the sofas that had been strategically positioned around a small platform. Full-length mirrors curved along one side.

Blue was right, this place felt lush.

I took a bite of a sandwich just as Jemma turned to me.

"I hear you're dating Mac."

I choked, coughing through the lump in my throat. Honey handed me a glass of water, thumping my back. I swallowed, coughing once more to clear the blockage.

"Um, yeah. We've been together for..." I did the rapid calculation in my head and blinked. "Wow, it's been three months."

Collins' eyebrows rose. "No way has it been that long. You barely go three hours."

I redid the sums slowly, shaking my head. "No joke. Three months."

Blue swapped my water glass for a mimosa. "Here. You look like you need this."

I gulped the alcohol gratefully, stunned by the realisation.

Jemma smiled warmly, squeezing my hand. "I'm glad. That boy needs someone to love him."

Love!?

"Oh, I don't—" the denial caught in my throat.

Don't love him? Are you sure?

I busied myself with another sip of the delicious mimosa, desperate to cool the flush in my cheeks. Over the rim of my glass I caught Blue, Honey and Collins exchanging a knowing glance.

Bitches.

I couldn't be angry with them. We'd known each other for too long and been through far too much for me to hold their care against them.

But adoring my friends didn't mean I had to like them at this particular point.

Blue leaned in, her whisper low. "You want to talk about it?"

I shook my head, lifting my glass again. "Absolutely not."

Ella chose that moment to push back the curtains of the dressing room.

We all watched as she sashayed across the floor, coming to stand on the small platform.

Staring at my best friend as she swished her gorgeous dress from side to side, I felt like I'd been hit by a Mack truck.

Or, in this case, a *Mac* truck.

Oh, Gods. I love him.

Here, in this shrine to all things love, I could picture it. We'd elope because just the thought of planning a wedding gave me hives. I'd wear a gold and white saree; Mac would be in a suit. We'd get married in the mountains, somewhere remote where we could hide from the world, getting lost in each other for a full month.

We'd have kids. A pack of them because he wanted a soccer team, and I wanted noise and colour and sticky little fingers attached to tiny faces that kept asking for just one more cupcake.

We'd live in Capricorn Cove because that's where we fell in love. Or Cape Hardgrave, because that's where Mac was from. Actually, it didn't matter where we lived so long as we were together and he loved me.

And he does. He loves me.

"Ani?" Ella called, holding her arms out and striking a pose. "What do you think?"

"I think I'm in love with Mac," I blurted out.

All heads swivelled from the bride to stare at me.

Shit. Oh shit. I've just ruined her day!

Ella rolled her eyes. "And you're just realising this now?"

I gulped, feeling as if my whole world were crashing down around me. "This isn't in my plans. He's completely shaken up my life, Ella. What do I do?"

Ella hiked up the dress, stepped down from the little podium and crossed to me. She pulled me up, wrapping me tight in her arms.

"You love him back. You tell him how you feel. You hold onto him, and you don't let go." She pressed a kiss to my cheek. "Put aside your fear, Ani. Love doesn't have room for doubts."

"I'm so sorry." I swiped at a stray tear. "Talk

about a maid of honour fail. I'm ruining your day."

She shook her head. "Nope, not a word of apology out of you. Love doesn't have a timeline. When you know, it just hits you. Thank you for letting me be a part of this moment."

I shuddered, more tears burning the back of my eyes. "You look beautiful, my wise friend."

She laughed, pushing me away and smoothing the skirt of the dress. "I hate it. This isn't me."

It's true, a princess cut that drowned her in a million layers wasn't anything like what Ella would or should wear.

Yasmin, sensing the change, sprang forward.

"Let's try something different, shall we?" She led Ella away, leaving me with the other women.

Blue handed me a tissue. "You okay?"

I nodded, dabbing at my eyes. "Sorry," I apologised to the group. "I didn't mean to lose it like that."

Liv waved me off. "Don't sweat it. Weddings bring out the crazy in all of us. I should know. I worked on the set of *Just Married* for three years."

I blinked. "The arranged marriage reality tv show?"

"Uh-huh." She nodded. "Pure batshit crazy

in a can. Honestly, all we needed to do was put those people in a room, and they went bananas."

"Didn't two of them work out?"

She laughed. "Some of them always work out. And they're always the ones who believe in true love."

"So, the moral is, believe in love?" Honey asked.

Liv shrugged. "But of course."

Ella tried on a pin-up, which was nice but not perfect. A boho wispy dream followed, which made her look like a plump sugar fairy and a mermaid dress that threatened to spill her boobs at the slightest move.

"Gunnar would approve of that one!" I cat-called, clinking my glass with a laughing Blue's.

On the tenth unsuccessful dress, Yasmin took over, pulling three dresses from the racks and vetoing all our previous selections. She emerged from Ella's dressing room, a pleasant flush on her cheeks.

"Ladies, I don't want to jinx us, but I think we found *the dress*," she whispered, frantically pulling various accessories from hangers and drawers before running back into the dressing room.

"I remember this," Collins murmured. "Finding the right dress sucked."

I raised an eyebrow. "When did you get married?"

She flushed, dropping her head. "I meant when I went through this with Emily," she said, referring to her sister. "It was a nightmare. She tried on something like five hundred dresses before settling on one."

"Let's all pray that doesn't happen this time round."

Ella emerged a few minutes later, beaming as she stepped toward us.

The dress wasn't at all what I would have picked for her. It wasn't pin-up, nor was it beach boho. It was a mixture of the two.

Lace decorated the top of the gown, ending just below her elbows. A corset silk bodice cupped her breasts, flaring at her hips to give way to pure silk. The silk hugged her curves all the way down to the floor, where it brushed gently in a soft whisper of movement. Lace lay over the top of the bodice and met a chiffon float of material at the bottom.

Yasmin had added a contemporary cape and woven through Ella's hair a crown made from leaves, fake flowers, and silver.

"Oh, Ella..." Her mother breathed, tears shimmering on her lashes. "Baby, you look magnificent."

In hushed awe, we watched as Ella glided

up to the podium, coming to stand before the mirrors. She gently moved this way and that, giving herself a satisfied nod.

"Perfect," Yasmin declare, fluffing out the short train. "We'll add the cape because it's an outdoor wedding in Autumn, and it'll get cool during the reception. I wouldn't recommend it during the ceremony because we want to show off the beautiful gown. If you want a veil, I can make it work, but I'd really suggest we source you an elegant but subtle headpiece."

Satisfied she'd adjusted the dress, she stepped back, surveying her handwork. "What do you think?"

Ella turned, her face carefully blank as she looked at us. "Thoughts?"

"It's perfect!"

"If you don't get it right now, I'll murder you."

"Gunnar is going to lose his mind."

We talked over each other, gushing at her beauty. Ella's eyes met mine, tears shimmering on her lashes.

"I'm getting married."

I nodded, a hitch catching my breath. "And your husband is gonna lose his fucking mind when he sees you in that dress."

She laughed, the tension breaking as she rapidly brushed at her face. "God, look at me.

Never have I ever thought that I'd be a crier-bride. At this rate, I'll have to swap my bouquet for a tissue box."

Then Yasmin said the magic words that cemented this as the dress of the decade.

"If you're worried about crying on the day, the dress has pockets. You can tuck a few handkerchiefs in there."

"Oh, my Gods! Buy it now!" Liv cried, her hands flying to her chest. "Pockets!"

"Whoever made this dress is a goddamned saviour," Honey declared.

"Whoever made this dress had to be a woman. Only women understand our pocket desire," Blue added.

Ella laughed, turning to the assistant. "Thank you, Yasmin. I'll take it."

While Ella got changed and went through the measurement routine for her order, I walked through the store, fingers gliding over the pretty dresses, considering the changes the last year had brought for our lives – Ella getting married, our little bar turning a decent profit, Mac.

Today was the beginning of the next stage of my life.

Now I just needed to tell Mac.

13

Anika

I swallowed nervously, running sweaty palms down my leg.

I'd taken the day off and spent most of it cooking. The fruits of my labour had been carefully transported down to the marina, laid out on eight tables stretching from one side of the boardwalk to another, each dish covered by a silver cloche.

I could hear Gunnar's laughter and Mac's deep voice as they rounded the building. Butterflies took flight, morphing into pterodactyls as I caught sight of Mac.

Here we go.

Ella, Honey, Collins and Blue lined the boardwalk, politely but firmly turning any stray walkers away. Tonight, this section was just for Mac and me.

He stopped, taking me in, his gaze slowly starting at the sexy as fuck heels on my feet, the black straps wrapping seductively around my ankles, up my bare legs to the dress that hit me at mid-thigh. His perusal continued up across my belly, where the thin fabric clung suggestively. He lingered on my cleavage, which I'd pushed up to full advantage, then took in my hair and then finally met my gaze, his lips quirking.

"What's with the domed silver tray cover thingys?"

I spluttered, my hand automatically reaching out to swat him. "They're called cloches, you uneducated buffoon!"

He chuckled, the rich sound turning me into a warm puddle of needy goo.

"I take it we've got plans?"

I swallowed, nodding.

Gunnar clapped him on the shoulder and turned, taking up guard at the end of the boardwalk.

Mac approached, holding out a hand for me to take. I latched on as if my life depended on it.

You can do this, Anika. You got this.

I led him up the boardwalk to the first cloche, placing my hand on the lid.

"Pay attention, MacDaddy, there will be a quiz at the end." I lifted the silver dome revealing a margarita.

He laughed, giving my hand a squeeze.

"The first time I met you, I drank a margarita, and you kissed salt off my lips."

I picked up the glass to take a sip. I then tilted my head, and Mac grinned, cupping my jaw to kiss the salt from my lips.

"Yeah," I whispered. "Just like that."

"Mm, I think I like this game."

I led him to the second cloche, revealing a fat eggplant.

He stared at it blankly. "Um, not sure I get this reference, babe."

"The second time we met, I asked Jack to order aubergines. Just keep in mind that I know them as aubergines, as in 'A', not eggplants, as in 'E'."

He nodded, his brow furrowed slightly.

"I threatened you with a knife, then agreed to let you move in," my lips quirked. "You gotta be prepared for that kind of whiplash in the future, okay?"

His eyebrows rose, and I could see him starting to put together what I was doing. I grabbed his hand, quickly dragging him to the third table, a jar of Reese's peanut butter.

"The day you moved in, I was making pie.

Instead of saying it was perfect, you suggested salt. I knew then that you were a foodie and someone who would appreciate my culinary efforts."

"I appreciate everything you do, Anika." His growled, his voice rough with emotion.

The fourth dish was a Rueben sandwich.

"That was the day when everything changed. I couldn't fight my attraction."

He pulled me close, pressing hot kisses to my mouth. "You still can't."

I chuckled, nervous excitement now simmering through my veins. He backed me up to the next table, kissing me the entire way.

"Fifth," I said breathlessly, breaking away from him. "Yellowfin tuna."

"From the dinner with your parents."

I nodded, swallowing. "And the first night you said you loved me."

His restraint broke. He pulled me to him, devouring my mouth, his tongue hot and wet and perfect as it teased and tasted mine.

With effort, I pulled away, leading him to the final three cloches.

I pulled the cloche off the first one, revealing a mimosa.

"Sorry, Ani. Not sure I remember that one."

"You wouldn't. You weren't in the bridal store yesterday when I had my epiphany."

"Epiphany?"

I shook my head, dancing away from his reaching hands and lifting the seventh dome.

"Eggs?" Mac asked, crossing his arms over his chest.

I nodded, gesturing at the final and largest cloche. "You can lift that one."

He did so slowly, revealing an elaborate miniature three-layer wedding cake. On the top was a simple question mark made from chocolate.

His body froze.

"Tell me about the mimosa and eggs," he ordered.

"At the wedding dress store, they served us mimosas. I had just taken a sip when Ella walked out of the dressing room looking like a bride."

"A terrible one!" Ella called from her position on the boardwalk. "The dress was hideous."

I laughed, loving the grin that lit Mac's face. "But even looking hideous, seeing her like that, shopping for the dress she'd marry Gunnar in, it hit me."

My courage fled as I stared into his eyes, suddenly unable to continue.

Mac stepped forward, pulling me against him, cupping my jaw as he searched my face. "It hit you?"

"I love you," I whispered. "And I want to marry you. I want the wedding and the house, I want nights with you, and I want kids. I want days on boats, and I want pets. I want it all. I want you."

He swallowed, his voice deep and raspy as he asked, "And the eggs?"

I huffed out a wet laugh. "I could lie and say it's because I want to eat eggs with you every morning, but really, I just needed a food that started with an 'E'."

He frowned, and I saw the exact moment he deciphered my coded message.

"Yes," Mac breathed, scooping me up and swinging me around. "Fucking hell, yes!"

He kissed me as if he were drowning and I was air. He touched me as if he would never stop.

Behind us, I heard Gunnar ask Ella what happened.

"Think about it, Viking. Margarita, Aubergine, Reese's peanut butter, Rueben, Yellowfin, Mimosa, Eggs, and a cake with a question mark. What's the first letter of each word spell?"

"M, A, R, R – holy shit. She asked him to marry her!"

"Yeah, babe. Took you long enough."

Mac abruptly let me go, dropping to his

knees and scrambling for something in his pocket.

"Mac, what are you--?" I choked, my eyes no doubt as big as plates as I stared at the little box in his hand.

"Holy shit, this is a plot twist I did *not* see coming," Blue whispered behind me.

"Anika Livia Sharif, even though you've stolen my thunder—"

I laughed at his outrageous statement.

"—I need to ask; will you wear my ring?"

I brushed tears away, nodding frantically. "Yes!"

He surged up, slipping the ring on my finger with shaking hands, and then kissed me.

"Do you think this means he's staying?" Gunnar asked. "Cause I could really use the help. This marina is a fucking mess."

We broke apart, heads still pressed together, arms wrapped tight, bodies shaking as we laughed.

"I love you," Mac said, brushing his fingers across my cheek.

"I love you too."

"You good if I take you to the boat to ravish rather than home? It's closer."

I laughed, joy spilling free. "Sounds perfect."

EPILOGUE ONE

Mac

Sometime in the near future...

I put my hands on my hips, lifting an eyebrow as I stared at the giggling gaggle of women in the lock-up.

Ani, seeing me staring, shot me a saucy look. "Hey MacDaddy, you here to bust us out?"

The women fell over each other, laughing as if this was the most hilarious moment of their life.

I glanced at Sheriff Tristan Rodriguez. "How long have they been in there?"

He looked amused. "About an hour."

I looked back at my soon-to-be wife. Her sash was half falling off, her crown crooked. She was three sheets to the wind, with glassy eyes, and a flushed face.

I wanted to kiss the breath out of her.

"How much is bail?"

The Sheriff waved me off. "Nothing. We just needed them to dry out a little. Pretty sure my wife is as pickled as the rest of them."

It was only after he mentioned his wife that I surveyed the other women in the room.

"If she's a good girl will you bail her out?" Liv yelled, doubling over with laughter before sliding off the bench and landing on the floor, setting the women off into peals of hysteria once more.

"Jesus." I ran a hand over my face. "Liv's husband is gonna be mighty pissed with me."

"Nah. This is nowhere near as bad as that time when we all—"

I grimaced, shaking my head and cutting off Liv's drunken retelling. "I doubt any of us will forget that trip." I turned back to the cell. "Okay, up you get ladies, let's go. Single file."

I took them outside to the waiting limo, helping them as they stumbled, collecting discarded shoes along the way.

The driver had the decency to look ashamed. "Sorry dude, they just didn't stop."

I shook my head. "Just take them back to our place."

I followed in my car, mentally cursing the next few hours. No doubt there would be multiple trips to the toilet, a few who wanted to keep the party going, and at least one who'd try to make a break for it when my back was turned.

Sleep is overrated, right?

I stood at the kitchen counter the next morning, buttering toast and serving coffee when Anika emerged from our bedroom. Her hair was a mess, she still had last night's makeup smudged across her face, and she smelled slightly of stale beer.

And she remained the most beautiful woman I'd ever seen.

"Hey, MacDaddy." She lifted on tiptoes, pressing a quick kiss to my cheek. "Sorry about last night."

"It was all Liv's fault," Blue said from her spot at the breakfast bar. She'd taken my offered painkillers, downed them then rested her head on her arms. She had yet to do more than moan every now and then.

"Liv?" I asked.

"Yeah, since she stopped breastfeeding three weeks ago, she decided to go all out." Anika winced. "We may have tried to keep up."

"Speaking of Liv, where is she?" I asked, glancing around.

"The woman doesn't get hangovers. Her husband picked her up an hour ago. I expect they're returning to the hotel for monkey sex before flying out," Blue answered, her voice dripping with annoyance.

I nudged the painkillers in Ani's direction. "Toast will be ready in a moment, Chef."

She grinned and then winced, taking the seat next to Blue.

We weren't due to fly out for our elopement for another two days. And then it would be all Ani, all the time.

I couldn't fucking wait.

But first, her friends had insisted on throwing her a bachelorette party.

That was your first mistake. Your second was waiting a full year before marrying the love of your life. Your last was allowing Liv to plan the party.

I'd known Liv my whole life – the woman was certifiably crazy and motherhood hadn't done anything to blunt her crazy tendencies.

"Hey, Ani?"

She looked up from the coffee cup she'd been staring into for the last five minutes.

"Love you."

Her beautiful grin was instantaneous and as breathtaking as ever. "Love you too."

And all was right in my world.

EPILOGUE TWO

Anika

"God damn it," I groaned, ignoring the Braxton-Hicks contraction. "My back is killing me."

"Well, you are overdue by three days," Blue pointed out. "You could pop at any time."

I covered my stomach with both hands. "Hush your mouth! Knowing my luck, he'll hear you and decide this is the moment to appear."

As if to give evidence to my concern, the baby in my belly kicked, his little foot connecting with where I lay my palm. I'd never get tired of feeling that connection. Three babies later, and I still got shivers every single time.

"I still think it's a girl," Ella said, reaching out to pat my stomach. "And you'll be named after me, won't you little princess?"

I laughed, shaking my head. "It's a boy. After three sons I've given up hope of a female to even the number."

I groaned, rubbing my back as another Braxton-Hicks hit me.

"You know, I'm sure Farrah would have organised for a private performance if you'd asked," Ella commented, sipping her glass of wine.

"Yeah, but they're so rarely in town these days that I prefer them to spend family time with us as a family – not performing because I can't get my cankle-y butt to a stadium."

Ella rolled her eyes. "It's her husband's *job*, Ani. And he loves it. He's not gonna say no to the mother of his nephews."

It was true, my sister had chosen a good man to marry – that he was a world-famous rock star was just a minor detail. His crooning voice had rescued me at bedtime more than once. His voice didn't lose its appeal even when on a video call.

A roadie stepped up on stage, a hush immediately falling over the crowd in the Bronze Horseman.

"Ladies and gentlemen, may I introduce, Farrah and –"

I yelped, liquid gushing down my legs as my water broke.

"Oh fuck," Ella laughed from beside me as people immediately began to shift, responding to my distress. "I guess you were right. This bubba did hear me."

"You bitch." I glared in her direction then looked around the crushed bar for Mac. "You better call for a clean-up on table five. Mac-Daddy is gonna lose his shit if I'm not out of here in the next few minutes."

Our third son had arrived less than an hour after my water had broken. We'd just made it to the hospital. Mac refused to take chances with son number four.

"So those *were* real contractions." Mac sat his beer down on the table, clucking his tongue. "I told you."

"Oh hush," I ordered, reaching out my hands to him. "Help me up and let's get this over with."

He pulled me into his arms as the event staff rushed around clearing a path for us to leave.

"You really know how to shake things up," Mac laughed, lifting me into his arms with a little grunt.

I pressed a kiss to his cheek. "Well, you started it."

He stopped, looking down at me, his precious face carved with joy. "And thank the Gods you let me."

Forty-three minutes later, our lives were

shaken up once again as we met our fourth baby and first girl, Asha Ella Mackenzie.

~

I adored writing Mac and Anika! Honestly, they were just a delightful pair who I couldn't help but delight in! I sincerely hope you loved them as much as I do.

If you loved this book, be sure to check out the next in the Capricorn Cove series. Double the D features Blue and some delicious blasts from her past.

You can continue the entire series by checking them out on my website at
www.EvieMitchell.com
If you enter the code EBOOK10 you can get 10% off your purchase from my website.

ALSO BY EVIE MITCHELL

Capricorn Cove Series

The Shake-Up

Double the D

Muffin Top

The Mrs. Clause

New Year Knew You

Double Breasted

As You Wish

You Sleigh Me

Resolution Revolution

Meat Load

Larsson Siblings Series

Thunder Thighs

Clean Sweep

The X-list

Reality Check

The Christmas Contract

Dogg Pack Books

Puppy Love

Bad English

The Frock Up

Pier Pressure

All Access Series

Knot My Type

Love Flushed

Nameless Souls MC Series

Runner

Wrath

Ghost

Shield

Elliot Security Series

Rough Edge

Bleeding Edge

ABOUT THE AUTHOR

Evie Mitchell is a thirty-something romance author (she/her/hers) living with disability. She believes in inclusion, accessibility, and fierce romance. Her loves include steamy romance novels, her husband, their THREE sausage dogs (heaven help her), and her ever-growing collection of book-related mugs.

As a woman with a diverse work history including in areas such as emergency response, event management, human rights, disability access, and security - her books are filled with true stories (bridezillas), worst-case scenarios (malfunctioning dresses), and her favorite tropes (one-bed).

Evie specialises in fiercely inclusive happily ever afters.